30 Years
of Publishing

LANZMANN

AND OTHER STORIES

LANZMANN

AND OTHER STORIES

DAMIAN TARNOPOLSKY

Exile Editions

30 YEARS OF PUBLISHING

2006

Library and Archives Canada Cataloguing in Publication

Tarnopolsky, Damian

Lanzmann and other stories / Damian Tarnopolsky.

(Add line here)

ISBN 1-55096-078-4

I. Title.

(Add line here)

Design and Composition by Homunculus ReproSet
Cover Painting by Harold Bräul
Typeset in Galliard and Akzidenz Grotesk at
  the Moons of Jupiter Studios
Printed in Canada by Gauvin Imprimerie

The publisher would like to acknowledge the financial assistance of
The Canada Council for the Arts and the Ontario Arts Council.

Conseil des Arts   Canada Council
du Canada   for the Arts

ONTARIO ARTS COUNCIL
CONSEIL DES ARTS DE L'ONTARIO

First published in Canada in 2006 by Exile Editions Ltd.
RR#1 Gen. Del.
144483 Southgate Road 14
Holstein, Ontario, N0G 2A0
info@exileeditions.com
www.ExileEditions.com

Sales Distribution:
McArthur & Company c/o Harper Collins
1995 Markham Road, Toronto, ON M1B 5M8
toll free: 1 800 387 0117   fax: 1 800 668 5788

For Kate

CONTENTS

THE LANZMANN QUARTET
IN PITTSBURGH

After the scene at the airport it was necessary for me to meet with Franz's wife. "To clear the air," I said when I telephoned her room, trying to put it in words she would understand. I had to meet with her, with this woman who had been campaigning against me since she'd seduced Franz, who had been leading him away from me, putting mediocre ideas in his head, insinuating herself gaudily into our relations. When she married him matters became impossible, in all the ways I'd predicted in the speech I gave at their hideous, tasteless wedding. This woman—this shrill woman, with her delighted ignorance of music, her garish "business" attire, her banal mental processes, her blind stupid youthful American optimism—this woman planted herself on stage when we rehearsed, scowling when I corrected her husband on this or that phrasing gaffe or blundering fortissimo, crossing her long arms, sighing.

Franz had started making ridiculous suggestions, in her voice— *Let's contemporize our repertoire; Let's begin a festival.* She sent me faxes in her disturbing insane scrawl, faxes Franz signed in his gentle round hand, screeds insisting on some ludicrous exploration of new venues, a new record label. She fancied herself an administrator, and had proposed to take over the group's administrative duties—bookings, tour arrangements, all the things our agents would have done if we had not been abandoned by two agencies in eight months. "Administrative duties": she was proposing, that is, to take the keys to the kingdom, the pursestrings, Authority, away into her glossy mitts. I rejected that out of hand. But she insisted on travelling with us, and this was unheard of. Claude and Johann are unmarried, naturally; neither of my ex-wives was invited along on tour—I wouldn't have invited them when we were still married either. I never had. There is a reason an army travels without its women. She was destroying us. Franz had become her puppet. She was twenty years younger than him. She wanted to make her way in the world. I wanted to fuck her until her brains came out of her ears.

I'd confronted Franz, bland, pudgy, bearded Franz, about it, about this ludicrous idea of hers, this idea of travelling with us, and with Franz I was used to getting my way. But he hemmed and hawed, tears softened the triangles of his eyes. *It's our honeymoon, if you like*, he said. I put my foot down: it was obvious to me she was trying to undermine my leadership, trying to worm her way in, in the worst way, trying to displace me from the quartet I had established, which bore my name: *Lanzmann*. When I next saw Franz he was full of spirit, he had spoken to his wife, but I would not be moved. And so she travelled along behind us, with us but not with us. She accompanied the tour but she was not part of the tour. She took the same flight with us from Chicago to Pittsburgh, but she was not seated with us. She sat at the back of the plane. Franz grudgingly went back to visit her and then returned to play euchre with Johann and Claude, the two old biddies, my viola and my cello. I ignored them, writing a letter instead to the conservatory complaining about the incompetence of the students they'd sent me this semester.

So we arrived in Pittsburgh—Claude had made us late with the customary cello/national security rigmarole—and I found the driver the hall had sent and he led us to his minivan, telling us in the meantime what a fine hotel we were staying at, what a fine city Pittsburgh was. I lifted my lapels against the brushing of the snow. As we stowed the suitcases in the van's open jawbone we could see

Christina a hundred metres ahead of us, waving desperately for a taxi and finding none. And with the snow starting to pummel down, she saw us. The biddies, taking their comfortable seats, cello case between them, murmured. Franz raised himself to his fat height. She walked determinedly towards us. The scene ensued.

"I'm really so glad you wanted to meet," she said, in the evening, bathed, fed and settled, sitting delicately to my right in the hotel bar. I could see us both in the mirror above the bourbons. My hair shone; we looked like a couple preparing for a secret night in from the cold, an executive and his gorgeous personal assistant: he is at a conference; she travels with him everywhere; she pours herself another glass of wine. Yes. It struck me that for the most part she does herself no justice: this short hair she keeps, with just blotches of blonde, the rectangular overcoat she wears that covers her curves. Because she has rich features, her skin beams, she takes pleasure in the world. I wondered how an elephantised milquetoast like Franz, a giant soft fleshy woman-man, how did Franz manage to engrip a cheerleading champion, a younger, healthier, small-town Americana businesswoman? What on earth did he say to her?

"I'm so glad you wanted to meet. Look. First thing I want to say is, I'm sorry about this afternoon. I know you are too. I was angry with you and you were angry with me and you know what? That's okay. It's okay to be angry. Because we both want the same thing. We both want the Lensmin quartet to achieve greater success. We're just coming at this from different angles."

The barman came. She ordered a gin and tonic. I asked for the same.

"Two gin and tonics."

"Better make it four," I corrected, and he nodded. "I hate to wait," I told her.

Immediately he had the drinks ready.

"I know it's weird for you. I know me being here is weird for you. But I want to make it work, you know? I have a few ideas, you know?"

"Not just a pretty face," I said.

"I've worked in orchestras. I played flute with the San Diego orchestra for two years, remember? And I've worked as an agent. I went to school and I studied this. When we met I told you all my ideas and you said you wanted to hear me out. So hear me out, you know? That's all I'm saying."

Her voice was attractively brittle. I must have seemed to turn away because she pulled at my sleeve.

"Listen, Cesar, you don't have time to lead the group, and be manager and agent as well as teach and practice and write—it's too much for anyone. I want to help out. I can help out administratively, I've already offered to do that. But you know what? I'm more ambitious than that. I think Lensmin can take off. I think in two years we could become the biggest thing on the circuit—you've got the talent. We all know that musically you're a genius. It's just a management question."

I didn't like her using my first name. I was looking at her thighs and wrists.

"Here's my idea. I think the management of this whole operation needs to be more fluid. More democratic, if you like. There are ideas across the whole group that need to be aired. Franz is full of ideas. Claude and Johann are really thoughtful men when you sit down to talk to them, you know?"

She took a minuscule sip of her drink.

"Look," she said.

With a ballerina's reach she curled down to an attaché case at the feet of her barstool, and I saw the sunrise of the taut skin of her lower back, between the black cashmere that was rising and the pants that stayed fixed in place tightly round her waist. She was looking for something in her leather bag. I like to see a woman's back stretch and return, the muscles abduct, I know what it reminds me of. She'd been a gymnast at college, no, a volleyball player, I decided; she wore light-blue camisoles to bed, she could scuba dive, she bought her perfume in airports. Doubtless. But imagine what she could *do* with those haunches. She curled back up again and turned the stool round bright-faced and gave me a red vinyl folder.

A transparent sheet and a title page: *Rebranding the Lanzman Quartet—Let's Hit a High Note Together*. I read this aloud, gingerly, because I have never liked the sound of my English voice.

She smiled eagerly. "Take a look through," she said. "Don't tell me what you think yet. Just think about it."

A pie chart. New Markets. Strategic Tactics. A page of Success Descriptors. A huge treble clef with a thick blue arrow pointing away from it to a dollar sign. Curiously I had never noticed the resemblance before.

I finished my second weak gin and tonic.

At the back of the folder were some notices: the San Francisco paper praising my adventurous playing and defiant originality; the *Tribune* on my "almost sculptural depth of tone." Fortunately she'd blacked out the part where that bastard Nilbuhr called me "an uncareful presence." I'd make him pay for that yet.

"Excellent," I said. "Excellent excellent."

I leaned in and patted her knee.

"Tell me," I began, looking up from the folder.

"Shoot," she said, smiling, hopeful.

I moved my hand up the denim of her thigh. I could see the first lines above her cheek.

"When Franz fucks you from behind," I asked, "does he hold you by your hips, like this? Or does he lean forward over you and grab your breasts? Because that's what I would do. I'd lean right over you and hold on to them, fucking you. Until you screamed."

• • •

In my room I took off my suit pants and left them in the press and was kneeling in my undershorts in front of the minibar, waiting for my sandwich to arrive. The tour was turning into a disaster. We had been playing poorly; we had lost a dimension of understanding; I felt like an officer whose conscripts mill about as he leads them over the top. Even ordering a sandwich had been almost impossible, room service insisting they had no such thing on the menu, that it was too late, until I demanded of the manager if he was running a hotel or a south Asian prison. The screaming damaged my throat. Finally I ripped the phone from its socket and threw it at the wall, where it left a crater, and I waited.

I have never been allowed to become what I desired to be. My whole life I have been sabotaged by the people around me. Franz's wife was just the latest. The quartet, which I established, has never reached the standards I set us. When we left the orchestra I had high hopes, the highest hopes. But the men around me proved weak and so it would always be. Victor had no ideas. Roland was unorthodox. Heinrich was at first technically brilliant, but as time passed he grew lazier and lazier. Anton was a good soul, very musical, but he always wanted the stability of being second violin in some provincial string section. None of these people stayed with me, so we developed no consistency. And yet each unit I put together, in each unit there was immense potential— we could have been among the great. We had the talent—but they always let me down.

And now Franz, Franz who has been ballooning out so, who has become given more to eating than to performing. Whose art has lost its definition as his body has gained bulk. His wife is trying to prise us apart—just as I have put together a unit, with Franz and the two biddies, that has variety, stability, flair, understanding. Just as I have done this, she has come to destroy us. Now Franz leaves me too.

A light double knock at the door, my sandwich, interrupted these joyful thoughts.

It was a boy of twenty, healthy-looking, broad-shouldered, cupboard-shaped, freckle-faced. Wearing a blue sweatshirt with a tartan M embroidered into it. I looked up at his flat friendly face and he looked down at my bare legs. He was carrying a violin case—my heart sank, he probably wanted me to audition him, it happens every week—the handle hooked on one finger.

"You don't have my sandwich," I said.

He laughed nervously, with a thick-jawed smile. "No?"

"Then fuck off."

I kicked at the television and found the news. When the commercials came on I heard another knock.

"For Christ's sake," I said, because he hadn't moved. I looked down the hall for my food.

"I'm sorry Maestro, I tried to call, but your phone isn't working. They told me just to come up because you're leaving tomorrow. I play," he said, angling the case up.

"Play what? Baseball? I don't care."

I started to close the door on him again, but the elevator pinged and a rolling white cart appeared, pushed by a Filipina. Heavenly. I signed the yellow form and waved the cart away. "Take him too," I said to her, and turned round, took a bite of the sandwich. Shaved lettuce fell on to the floor.

"Wait," he said.

I licked some mustard from the side of my mouth and went to ass-push the door closed behind me.

"I'm Julietta Rodrigues' son."

So I looked at him again, slowly. I looked hard for her face in his; I looked for her green eyes and characterful hard nose and dismissive perfect mouth and sleek neck. I remembered her face. I couldn't see the resemblance. A quick calculation: I'd met Julietta Rodrigues fifteen years before. Sixteen? For five years on my visits to the Florida Festival I buggered her in every hotel room in Miami. The boy was at least twenty, he must be. She was married but she'd never mentioned a son.

"My mom said I should come to see you once. She spoke about you a lot. She had all your recordings."

That made me smile.

"What's your name, son?"

"Alvaro," he said.

"You look more like a Chip or a Chet. Well, come on."

Sandwich and boy came in.

For an hour or two I entertained him, trying to dissuade him from a life in music, and telling him about touring, about British food and Moroccan women. I didn't tell him his mother had an ass like two tennis balls in plastic wrap, like two whale's eyes, he probably knew that already. I told him about the great violinists and Haydn's mistake and the scandals students like to hear about. If it were up to me, I told him, all other quartets but my own would be destroyed, their recordings erased.

His voice descended a half-tone when I asked him about his mother. She'd died two years before. Forty-seven years old, she dropped dead of an aneurysm in the street. This woman who'd sucked me off with frozen grapes in her mouth.

8

"Life's a war," I told her son. "Music's war."

He nodded. He was sitting on the bed. My chair was at the dark wooden desk, the empty plate, the green leather blotter, the lamp. I went to get us another vodka from the mini-bar.

"So what's that thing for?" in my socks I kicked at his case.

"I hoped I might play for you?" he said sweetly.

"No way. Not now."

I laughed. But I liked him. I'd been earnest too, when I was his age. Tougher, but earnest too. I poured him his vodka and diet coke and came back with that and a tiny bottle of American whisky for me, and stretched my legs out.

"Before you leave then, Maestro?"

"We'll see."

Suddenly I was craving a cigar. I looked around the room.

"I won't waste your time." He'd laid the case down on the bed next to him and his fingers traced patterns on the bubbled black surface. "I'm at the faculty of music here." A gentle soul.

"The only good thing about a music school," I told him, "is that there are always twice as many women as men."

He actually blushed. I felt like I was falling for him.

"Who's your teacher?"

"Joseph Brugossian."

"Joey, Joey. A gambling man. Don't listen to anything he tells you about Mendelssohn."

"Okay, Maestro," he smiled, looking down at his violin.

I hope Julietta died with that smile on her face, that red bloom. Perhaps she did.

"I wanted to do solo work. I don't want to get lost in an orchestra. But it's funny, just as you're here. I'm really getting drawn to quartet stuff. Professor Brugossian says it's the one medium where the sum is truly greater than the, I mean where the whole is truly greater than the sum of the parts."

I held my tongue.

"You've got less to work with than in an orchestra, okay? And it's not one instrument against the orchestra either. So everyone's involved equally, everyone has to pull their weight or the whole thing collapses. You know that feeling when you're in perfect synchrony, it's like rowing, the way the boat lifts when you're all making the same stroke at once, when you're all together; the boat sings."

He was talking about rowing.

I cleared my throat.

"Crotkin, at the Academy, he always used to tell me that I'd never be a great quartet player because of my personality. He said I was a showboater, he called me a Flash Harry, I didn't even know what that meant. He was my age and I was yours. Well, I proved him wrong."

"You studied with Crotkin?" he said softly, impressed.

Many years ago, I thought.

"He used to light a cigarette and hold it under my left hand, to make sure I kept my wrist high. He'd be so close I could smell the mothballs on his suit. On average, one of his students would commit suicide each year. But you cannot learn if you do not suffer."

He looked at me emptily.

"I'm going to practice now," I said, and I stood up and scratched at my balls. But he didn't move.

"My mom played me your discs when I was growing up. It's funny to meet you. I was seven years old and I wanted to play like you."

It was one in the morning, he was still sitting on the edge of my bed. He was a product of television. He talked about movies the same way, no doubt. He'd pulled the case on to his knees.

"I had this dream that we'd play together. You know that story they tell about Pinchas Zukerman? That's how I imagined it. I should have just done it, I should have come in playing, before drinking anything."

Pinky, I thought. Always bloody Pinky.

"How he was just a kid really and he went to see Perlman and the other two in their hotel room when they were touring and he said 'I want to play with you guys,' and they just laughed at him, they were world famous already, who's this kid? And he comes back and he says 'No really, I think we should play together,' and they laugh and send him away but he keeps bugging them and bugging them and finally they're like 'Okay, Okay,' and he comes to their room with this huge stack of music and they say 'You've got five minutes' and he starts to play and he plays for them in their hotel room for two hours and he blows them away. And that's how he got started."

He was fingering the case's golden buckles, pulling them open and flicking them shut. He looked up at me, feeling the moment, waiting for a Christmas present.

I yawned and patted him on the shoulder and slowly he stood up. At the door I told him "We've got rehearsal at four tomorrow. Come if you like."

"I will," he said, eyes suddenly fiery, and I felt like I saw her in his excitement.

Julietta Rodrigues, I thought.

•   •   •

Franz had been irritating me for the entire session. He had lost heart. In fact his heart was cosseted in layers of flabby pink flesh, American hamburgers and fatty acids. And Christina was filling his fat head with nonsense. He was full of love now; it made him impossible to work with.

We'd been at it for two-and-a-half hours, in ninety minutes we'd be on stage, but as I tried to perfect our performance he played spitefully, stubbornly. He avoided saying anything to me—obviously his wife had had words with him—and when I suggested a change he'd go along with it only as far as he wanted to: he played the first half of a bar legato, not the whole bar. He noted pedantically that his score was marked *molto allegro*, not *allegro*, so was I *quite sure* about the *allegro*, was my score perhaps marked differently, *hemm hemm hemm?*, looking to the biddies for a reaction. Such ego, such overweening ego, such a trivial way to express it. At least his wife had stayed away today, shopping no doubt, nursing her wounds in Macy's, bandaging them in yellow chiffon scarves.

The biddies lacked fire, as usual, but were otherwise competent. Stragglers from the theatre administration slipped in and out, tried to make themselves noticeable by tiptoeing down towards the stage. The sound in the hall was too clean: when there are no human bodies, no skin, no breath in the room, the sound reflects off metal and bright wood. And the heating was not on. We had already been interrupted twice, asked by the stage manager and then by the music director when we would be clearing the stage. There were lights to prepare, they had to move the piano off, etcetera.

Then Franz announced, in his mutinous new Bolshevik spirit, that he needed a break. That he had to rest if he was going to perform this evening, that it was absurd to go deeper and deeper into something that was already "as good as it is going to get," that he wanted to eat meatballs and prepare himself. The biddies blanched. It was only natural, he said, to rest, if he was going to be at his best. It had been too long a rehearsal already, he said; he was cold. And how many hundreds of times have we played the *Harp*, he said, and the Webern. We know our business, he said. The biddies leaned a touch closer together: it has always been the leader's prerogative to decide when we are prepared, to announce when we have done enough.

"This is strange, Franz," I said. "This is all very strange. These things you are saying, they are all rather strange, I think Claude and Johann would agree. We have a particular way of working, I believe, and this way of working has served us well, I think we'd all agree. And yet," I said, "You seem to be intent on sabotaging it and destroying us. They make me think Franz, your destructive, saboteur's acts, that there is some broader problem, some other aggravation that you are unable to express in any direct way, and so you make these comments, about your diminuendo, about your meatballs. You pick and scratch, you make your little saboteur's acts, rather than coming right out and saying what your problem is."

No one spoke.

"But really, Franz," I said, "You are seeing things upside down, or backwards. Because this problem that you have, it is not something in *us*, in the Quartet Lanzmann. It is something in *you*. We all know how you are slipping. We have all seen you slip. Johann practically had to slap you to prevent you from jumping through the coda in Michigan. Do you still practice, Franz? Are you practicing in your hotel room, or are you doing something else, with that little wife of yours? Because we've all noticed this decline in you, and I do not think it is just the decline of age. It is not just your weakening arms, your heaving belly. It is more than that.

"This obsessional eating, Franz. Of course you want to stop and eat now, of course you want to eat, not work—because this is what matters to you now, eating and drinking, potato fries and champagne, pork sausages. Because you are weakening, and you feel yourself weakening, and so you try to bulk yourself up, you try to strengthen yourself, and the more you strengthen yourself the weaker you become, the harder it is for you to lift your heavy limbs.

"In the andante Franz it's a *pizzicato*. How can you play a pizzicato, looking the way you look? It's like watching a hippopotamus dance, it's a ponderous clumsy bumping, I'm astonished, it is not like you. And yet when I try to point it out—when I try to point out that Beethoven said pizzicato, not 'obese lumbering oxen-hoofed clomping,' you resent me. You resent me for trying to improve us as a unit. Johann, Claude, have you ever heard as oafish a pizzicato as today? Of course not.

"Because there is something disgusting, Franz, in the way you slaver after that woman. Something indecent in a man of your age displaying such adolescent neediness. Trailing your arms on the ground after her. Prancing around behind her at her beck like a show horse. Your newfound ineptitude would be almost forgivable, Franz, if it weren't tied to this, this woman's constant, spiteful, unfounded attacks on us. On me, on Claude, on Johann. You side with her, Franz, because of this grotesque sexual passion you cannot keep to yourself. And your lack of integrity is destroying us, Franz. It is destroying this group. Destroying this quartet. I think you know what you have to do. I think I know what decision you have made. I think you should leave us now."

I felt I had handed him the revolver. I waited for him to use it. Instead there was a shout: Christina striding down the aisle.

"What are you doing?" she shrieked. "What do you think you're doing?" There was no other noise in the hall. Franz closed his mouth. I was standing, he and the biddies waited passively for Christina to arrive, like businessmen waiting for the 07:50. I turned to face her. For a long time there had been silence in the hall. The boy, Julietta's son, was looking up at me; two of the administrative staff who had come in again to remind us to hurry were standing at the back of the stalls, quite still.

"Ah," I said, "Our fifth member. Is she a cellist? Is she a soprano? No, a flute; we keep her in reserve."

14

"You can't do this." She had marched straight down to the front of the stage, ignoring the six steps at each edge. So she stood beneath us, her hands like two talons on the shining white wood.

"This is a management issue, and as far as I know I am still the manager of this group."

"You son of a bitch. You have a contractual obligation."

"Ah yes, she has an MBA. This is just what I was talking about, Franz."

"What are you going to do? Fire him?"

"You, madam, should shut your fucking mouth."

She drew back.

"Come on, Franz."

She walked back a few steps up the incline and turned and waited for him. For a moment there was hesitation on his part. His big white face was red and blotchy now, with anger or embarrassment. He stood up.

"You . . . you . . . Austrian," he sputtered at me, pointing with the bow.

In six slow paces he reached the steps. He had to pass in front of Johann and Claude but he ignored them. He turned to ease himself down each step, and Christina was several feet of carpet ahead of him, walking like a clockwork toy up to the exit. Then they were gone.

"Right," I said, gathering up my music from the stand. "Let's get dressed."

The seated biddies looked at each other.

"What if he doesn't come back?" murmured one.

"We'll have to cancel," said the other.

I had to speak to the director of programming.

Then walking out into the seats a sudden inspiration struck me.

"Allah will provide," I called out, and I intended to.

I walked briskly in the opposite direction to that which Franz had taken and on my way up the aisle stopped by Alvaro's seat, and bent towards him.

"We go on at eight," I whispered into his ear. "Wear a tux."

•   •   •

In my dressing room I opened my suit bag.

When I was a boy I went to concerts secretly, I would miss school to go to concerts the way other children went and smoked or played soccer in the square. Wednesday matinees, dress rehearsals . . . I would hide and stay for the evening performances. I wanted all the snobs in the audience to know that music was not their unique possession, that I would rise over them, look down, and destroy them. But it is essential to look the part. In my childhood fantasies I wore white tie and tails. Nowadays performers lounge on in sports jackets, and the women wear whatever they want. If I had my way this informality would be done away with: some things should be formal. In some things I am a traditionalist, I admit it.

I had less than an hour to prepare. The room itself, with footsteps audible through the ceiling, with chalk blue walls and a torn sofa and the smell that remains after flooding, was not a help. It was dark and too small for me and the mirror was smudged. I could hear the biddies talking next door. Still, I pulled my clothes out and laid them on the sofa and the plastic schoolroom chairs and stood before them naked.

Bettina, my first wife, was a minor countess, and she called herself a painter. She was looking for a career and she found me, and for a time I was her career. She was an aristocrat and I was a prodigy. She came to all my concerts and nodded dumbly out of time and in the intermissions I would fuck her in perfect four/four in a dressing room. We were just children. She loved rehearsal. I was in the orchestra too then, she loved watching us in our shirt-sleeves, in our corduroy trousers, wedding rings resting on music stands. She would bring a sketchbook: she drew us chatting to each other quietly as the conductor endlessly re-rehearsed the brass. She loved that we talked about sport, about films, not Tchaikovsky. She loved the sound of the orchestra stopping in parts like a machine breaking down when the conductor stopped us and not everyone had noticed. She was surprised that we played just as well out of uniform. But we don't, I would tell her, we don't.

First the undershirt. I had it made especially in Rome from a special soft, strong wool. The tailor put a belt round it like a thick apron string that you tie at the side—it moulds the lower chest, it gives a little extra support. When people come to a concert they come to a visual spectacle as well as an auditory one.

In vest and underpants I leaned into the mirror and gave my neck a few slaps of cologne, and took up my tools from the countertop. A little brush to bring out my eyelashes. Powder as a smoothing base. The thick red pencil so my lips don't disappear. Some bronzer, from a space age black cube, so my skin doesn't whiten under the lights. One thing I could never persuade the biddies of, or even Franz, was that in a hall a hundred metres long they had to give their features some definition, as an actor would. People want to see what they are hearing, I told them, but they mumbled evasively, as they did about everything else.

Bettina liked expertise and informality. She liked the moment when all the players are arriving, coming to the empty hall from different directions, in taxicabs and buses. I would be impatient to begin. She liked the laughter in between bars, the self-admonishing laughter when someone acknowledged a mistake. She liked musical jokes: I tell Roland to be a bit more *presto* and he starts two measures in to mock me. Musical jokes for musical jokers. She loved me. But she couldn't paint to save herself from drowning.

I slicked back my hair. I use the same gel my father did, but I use two coats of it, waiting ten minutes before the second, so that I properly shine. And looking in the mirror making a final inspection between sheens I thought perhaps it was time for more work to be done on my eyes. Something was leaving a line between my eyebrows, as if a knife had been drawn down between them; it made me look angry. Hair ready, I turned to the chair for the rest of my clothes. I pulled on the white shirt and made my bow tie perfectly, shimmied into the long black trousers, patent leather shoes. All this had been laundered at the hotel. A red cummerbund: one does not want to look too funereal, and it gives extra support. I spat twice into the sink.

Only when I was ready, I opened the case. She sprang into my arms from the green felt and nestled herself under my neck and I felt a kind of comfort from her ashy smell, her cherry-brown Cremona colour, her hips and lips. I let the air flow through her and around her and tightened her strings gently and held the bow above her for an instant, eyes closed, breathing her in.

I tuned up and played the theme from the Franck which had been in my head all day but that was all—I do not believe in excessive preparations. Either you are capable or you are not. I could hear the biddies grinding out their laborious scales in the dressing room they shared next door. There was a knock at the door and a young woman's voice: "Ten minutes, Maestro." I put on my black jacket and stretched my shoulders into it, and stepped out into the corridor.

Often you find that the more wonderful the auditorium the less impressive the backstage facilities, but in this case both were a disappointment. I saw "no smoking" signs and the inevitable union regulations affixed cheaply to the big white square bricks of wall. A long thin corridor with numbered wooden dressing room doors, and at each end a flight of steps. The fluorescent lights guarded by grilles. And there are always more people backstage than there should be: the stage manager's second cousin being shown around, some corrupt local grandee visiting before he falls asleep in a box. The boy tripped down the steps to my right. "I had some trouble getting past security," he whispered. We could hear the herded feet creaking their way into the auditorium above us. "I wish we could have rehearsed."

He looked a little pasty himself.

"There was no time," I told him, and led him in to meet the biddies.

Johann was standing tightly against a counter, Claude, unconcerned, sitting in a mouldering blue armchair reading the newspaper, cello case unopened upright next to him. He didn't look up. There was no space for us to manoeuvre. Johann took the boy's hand and the boy said he was honoured. Honoured to meet Johann.

"You're the one from the conservatory?" Claude said briskly. "The boy genius?"

Alvaro looked at me and I replied for him.

Claude asked, "When did you last play the *Harp*?"

A minim rest.

"We don't take the second movement too *lento*," Johann said to be conciliatory.

The boy excused himself and went back out into the corridor, to prepare, he said. He'd left his violin out there, carelessly—not a good sign. Claude shut the door and the biddies came to stand on my left and right. Johann held the viola with no hands above shoulder, as if an aspen post had been driven into his neck.

"What's the matter?" I began.

"This is ridiculous, ridiculous," said Claude.

"Ridiculous," Johann.

"We cannot possibly," said Claude.

"Can't possibly," said Johann.

"Have you heard him play?"

"This is ridiculous."

"Have you heard him play?"

"We cannot possibly."

"Have you heard him play?"

'Think of our reputation."

"We can't possibly."

"It's ridiculous, ridiculous."

"We have to cancel."

"We have to cancel."

"We have to cancel."

"Where is Franz?"

I raised my hands and they were silent. "Franz has gone," I began again. They started to speak and I cut them off by speaking over them, fortissimo. "Franz and Christine, exeunt. The boy's a prodigy. He's a gift to us." Their faces dropped, they looked sideways at each other for a beat, and then started again: "We have to cancel," "Our reputation." I let them continue for a while until both began to lose steam. Then I spoke confidently, authoritatively:

"Listen to me. Listen. We know the *Harp* backwards. I will lead the boy through the Webern. There is no issue. Listen to what you are doing. We were faced with a grave problem this afternoon, fruit of a crisis that has been coming for months. I saw it coming and I prepared for it, and I am trying to move forward. But instead of saying, Thank you for rescuing our concert, Thank you for spending the afternoon placating the program director, Thank you for spelling the boy's name to the printer, Thank you for making sure we'll actually get paid tonight—instead of this, you attack me, you attack me unceasingly, you criticize me, you doubt my good intentions. Would you rather leave with the oaf and his harpy wife? Go then. I'll play the fucking piece myself."

They hesitated.

I opened the door.

"Go on. Abandon me. Abandon all we've worked for."

They did not move.

Outside Alvaro was lying on his back spread out like a starfish, breathing in and out deeply with loud glissando sighs, moving his arms and legs in and out with each breath.

The young woman with red curls appeared again.

"Gentlemen," she said, and stretched out a welcoming arm towards the steps up to the stage.

I smiled. Johann lowered his viola into his arms.

"Get up," I said to the boy. "You'll get dust all over your outfit."

As we walked out on stage Claude made the sign of the cross. I nodded confidently to the boy, but he was pale. He gripped the violin hard at the neck, without any love or care, and marched with it like a baton. He paused, surprised apparently by the volume of the applause we were smiling at, and then unsure which seat to take. He moistened his fingers and turned the pages, stopped. We all looked at each other and he leaned forward and turned some more pages to another spot in the score. Ready, the three of us breathed in together; he was late to come in.

Musicians, like physicists, do their best work before the age of thirty—in many cases. So giving the boy this chance was not so great a gamble. Perhaps he was unused to performing in such a large hall; perhaps he'd done less chamber work than I thought; perhaps he'd lied to me about everything. In any case he made a noise that was like sandpaper rubbed against your face; with his bow he tried to saw through his strings. His fingers were hard; his back rocked back and forth stiffly and undifferentiated like a marionette's;

he didn't look up from his score—he didn't look at us for his cues. Claude firmed up the beat of the cello but it made no difference. The boy had waded in like a farmer walking into a fast-moving river, and he wasn't going to let anything distract him from getting to the other side.

Claude I could see was angry, his brow reddening. I wondered if he too would stand and leave, if he would even wait for the second movement. I felt the audience's energy drop. There had been tension in the room: any deviation from the programme, what I had called Franz's "indisposition," increases the audience's nerves. They want to know what's happening; they were excited about the debut of a "particularly gifted student." You could feel them deflate as the boy cudgelled his way through the adagio and we tried to build up a cushion around him. They could feel the back of their seats, their knees; they started to wonder if they'd make it to their restaurant tables in time. I suddenly had some respect for what Johann and Claude were doing, the perfect quiet lake they were charming into life together; and then the boy blundering over it raucously in his Sea-Doo.

In the pause between first and second movements, with a murmur in the crowd and the boy sweating, I knew it was up to me to rescue us, to provide the spectacular, as it always has been. I decided I would ignore the boy and play with the biddies as if this were our last concert together. There was only so much I could do: I would outdo him in volume, and I could try to cancel out his inadequacies by softening my arm, lightening my touch, by letting the strings sing with such beauty that it would absorb and negate his plucks and scratches. It required me to come in earlier than I was supposed to, to play over certain sections written for him, and it took some time for Johann and Claude to understand. Already with what the boy was doing the wheels were coming off—but I wanted the audience to take home if not a great concert at least one great performance.

I played as the part has never been played before, as Schup-panzigh himself would have dreamed of playing it, as the Creator heard it in his own head. I blocked out the boy's kicks and screeching stumbles and saw the platform Beethoven had laid for a soaring solo within this church he built. After a time I stopped hearing the boy; I heard the version of the piece as he could have played it only after years of work, if he'd been born a different person. I couldn't hear his failure, just the sound coming from my own shoulders, my chest, lifting me. I began to be excited.

Always I had felt hamstrung by those around me, but something astonishing began to happen. Always I'd felt like a three-legged dog, trying to run but hindered pock-pock-pock by wooden limbs. But now I felt I was lifting all four of us by my own playing, wings I'd made myself; even the boy was stimulated, rising up out of himself. I knew he could never rank with Franz, but I felt that lis-tening to me was bringing something out in him which not even he had known was there. The biddies I felt were floating with me, supporting me at last, as the four of us floated up like yogis an inch, then another inch off the floor.

We came to the end of the allegretto, to the brilliant flourish, and finished almost all together; the boy was only half a bar behind. There was silence, sudden silence. I looked at nobody, I was sweat-ing and exhausted. We had to go off for intermission. But I looked up at the audience and the silence continued. They sat still, and a panic flashed in my head: I didn't do enough, they hated me. And then I thought, No, No.

I remembered one of my childhood concerts, Klemperer con-ducting the Mahler *Resurrection*, and at the end of the piece there was none of the usual rhythmic applause. There was nothing at all. The old man looked down at the musicians arrayed around him in astonishment and turned to face the audience and there was a minute of silence and then another, and I looked around and asked myself, Why is no one clapping? And I realized that there were tears in the eyes of all the people around me; tears in my own eyes. They were so moved that they could not bring themselves to applaud, six hundred people sitting together too moved to applaud. It is what we wanted, I thought, it is what I always wanted. To reduce an audience to silence.

I looked at the boy and he was smiling like a child, immune to what he'd done. Johann and Claude were looking at the floor, awed. They couldn't face me. And so, alone, I stood up. The others stayed seated and I took a step away from my chair and stepped into the silence, and I bowed deeply, quickly, with passion. Nothing. I bowed again.

And then it began, with one man in the fifth row: a guffaw. Then a pause, and then another guffaw, something he couldn't restrain. And then a girl's high giggle simultaneous with an old man's bray, more of the guffaw, and these were the release for the rest. Laughter, and then there was laughter everywhere, cascading down from the balcony, from the boxes, washing up from the seats below me. I looked at Johann and Claude, practically curled up within their instruments. I looked out again and they were laughing, laughter in the stalls and laughter coming down from the gods. I wiped my face with my handkerchief and saw a little brown stain of bronzer and sweat. They made a noise like birds, a hurried inhuman shrieking, like a thousand programmes being torn up, like static. I could see chimpanzee mouths and immense teeth, guts in paroxysms, high notes and coughing. I looked back at the boy and he was smiling, I don't know why, his wide happy face exhausted and excited, and his lazy smile grew larger; and then he too began to laugh, with the rest of them.

SLEEPY

Perhaps it was my dad who brought me here. He would have stared ahead, hands like bunnies on the steering wheel. He stared ahead in the taxi, he stared ahead on the airplane, he stared ahead in the rental car, he stared ahead as I fetched my tiny turquoise suitcase. Did he look down to find the lever when he popped me the trunk? I don't know. I walked round to the driver's side window, and I gave him a dry kiss on the cheek. He drove away.

Sometimes in my bathroom the tiles jump up to meet me.

This is the story Lennie, a boy here, told me on the smoking patio. Dying I'd been to have a cigarette, this is what happens off Prixamil, and Lennie said "Smoking kills." I didn't know what he meant. The orange glow in your hands is enough for me. He said in his quick brown voice:

"This buddy of mine, his girlfriend won't let him smoke in their apartment, okay? Her cat's allergic or something. So every ten minutes he's out on the fire escape to smoke. Sneakers, jacket, snow, he sits on the iron grille legs poking out between the bars. He sees the backs of houses. Garages, vegetable gardens, the ash drops down between his feet four storeys down into puddles. His landlord's got a friend in the City, landlord sends this guy a crate of oysters every Christmas; so his landlord doesn't really do much in the way of upkeep, okay? Sometimes the balcony creaks and shakes in the rain. He hears it rattle. But he doesn't think anything of it. Plus he's got to smoke, okay? But one night he's out there and the wind blows and the screws give out and the whole damn thing collapses boom and he falls four storeys and the iron-work falls around him onto him and there you are."

I like oysters.

"Smoking kills."

I asked him, True story?

You open the curtain and pull it back. You fill your hair with conditioner. You wash your top half then your bottom half. Then stand under the water then stand under the water then stand under the water. Watching scenes in the warm water from last night's movie you saw half of. Waking up is a process of asking yourself questions, Dr. Frink says. Sometimes the questions don't come. The water's soft on my forehead, it runs down over my breasts and down over my thighs. A woman is banging on the door. An hour's passed.

Dr. Frink my shrink says I should engage with my surroundings. Otherwise I may persist in this belief that I am the sole moral arbiter of the universe. I don't really believe that, Dr. Frink, I'm pretty sure that you exist; I am just tired occasionally. My surroundings. There is a watercolour painting in my room of a boat tied to a very clean dock with a pebble beach in the background and a clubhouse and in pencil in very thin small caps beneath it is entitled *A Snug Harbour,* 121/450, Felicity Fitzgerald. I have stared at it for hours trying to work out what in god's name. The rest of the building, oh, I don't think I have patience for the rest of the building.

·   ·   ·

The rest of the building is also like a golf club. My dad would like it. Fat vertical lines of green and red and cream paper the walls. The couches are patterned with ducks and the one in the near social area is the least comfortable. There are corridors between the two social areas. One of the social areas has a television, the far one has a pool table. Off the corridors are everyone's rooms. It doesn't look like a hospital. No, it is not an asylum. There's too much wood here. But near each social area is a nursing station, just in case. Sometimes walking down the corridors you find pieces of medical apparatus that you've seen before but can't place. The men shuffle and hack. The social areas are very large like a swimming pool and divided into areas—dominoes, magazines, Monopoly—by wooden slats. Day and night I spend in my room. All my possessions fit into the top left drawer of the white dresser. There is an eighteen-inch screen television on it. The closet is empty. I do not have my own bathroom. I do not have a window. I feel tired all day and so woozy and I think probably I'll never have that feeling again of feeling *awake*.

Once in college before I dropped out the first time I was doing the dishes. I always did: I liked the chocolatey smell of yellow gloves and I'd put on the radio in the living room loud enough to hear over the water (Classical 93) and fill the sink. I liked it because I was washing up but also I was somewhere else, grocery shopping, talking to my sister Becky, making a list in my head of the clothes I would buy if I had money. Splooshing the sponge over the soup bowls, working, thinking of Lena Horne and my Portuguese chemistry teacher. Then Jennie my room-mate was yelling and only when she slapped me I woke up and the water was overflowing, there was foam all down my front and worst of all nothing was clean.

Lennie has big huge eyes that sit in wineglasses in his cheeks. He has dark insect hairs on his face but no stubble. He doesn't know how to laugh only a little; when he laughs he laughs with his whole chest. I think just possibly I am falling for Lennie.

I got pins and needles all over, I lost the sight in my head. I almost fainted again, thinking of that.

#24

LENA FEKE

CHECKLIST

Cataplexis (list triggers) :	4	(stress etc)
Somnambulism :	2	
EDS :	0	
Automatic behaviour :	2	
Food craving :	5	(olives)
Hallucinations :	0	
Nights of whole sleep :	7	
Nights of disturbed sleep :	1	
Hours of day sleep :	34	
Medication missed :	2	

Signature : _____

There are beautiful nasturtiums and hortensias in the gardens, and red walking paths. I'm finding myself there a lot. Also clay tennis courts. But best of all, towards the wall hedges on the far side of the gardens from the road, someone has built a Japanese garden. There are a thousand white-grey pebbles like the sea as its base. And low bushes growing out of the sea, and larger black rocks like shipwrecks. And I think that the moss growing on these rocks must be wet to the touch, but I don't want to walk out over the perfect engraved lines of the pebbles and ruin them, you great galoot. Actually I took ballet for nine years, I should give myself a little credit. The moss is the same colour almost as the round bushes, from the same square in the palette.

Would you believe that Lennie is a ventriloquist? The second week of October is National Ventriloquism Week. When he says these things, I . . . I don't know. He says that he is, however, an avant-garde ventriloquist. I said it was a lot of big words in a little sentence. It was like he was angry when he told me about his act:

"I don't understand why the only art that's stuck in the nineteenth century is mine. It's as if all painters were still doing water lilies. Listen. I do an act with a digital mike that makes you think the girl in the second last row is crying, okay? Even her mother turns to her. I make bikers sing nursery rhymes and tell me they love me. I do an act with a sex doll: it blows people away. Ventriloquism was originally associated with demonic possession. The only challenge is the illusion of action."

Okay.

All this happened in the medical staff cafeteria. I had never even been there before. I had not been exploring. I ate my bacon and eggs by myself or with Tom and Jerry, sitting in my bed, tray over my knees. My bed! Where else. It is the safest place for me and the warmest. But Lennie took me with him into the main building and down a flight of orange and brown stairs into the light blue basement ballroom where the doctors ate. He had on a labcoat and on it a blue badge said "ANDERS. VOLUNTEER." He told me he'd borrowed it. I bumped into the steel bars that you're supposed to slide your trays along and almost dropped everything. He had cannelloni stuffed with rabbit, which made me sad; I ate a salade niçoise. After, he played with the plastic tag around my wrist.

"Parts of a dream you remember and parts you don't," I said. Often I feel that when I'm talking in our little interviews it's not me talking but a different girl with my voice.

"What do you think you're getting out of this?"

I find Dr. Frink's beard distracting. It is mostly brown, with grey strands coming out of it. The beard is the dominant feature of his facial anatomy. It is immense, and without it I fear what would become of his physiognomy. If someone were to shave it off in the night.

"You don't have anything to say?"

I usually run out of things to say after about ten minutes. After that I struggle to stay awake. I think that's why he keeps talking, to keep me awake. And he tries to keep me talking. But it doesn't usually work.

"How are you finding the meals now?"

It was like he knew what we'd done.

We are sitting facing each other. Next to his elbow there is a small green sculpture of a polar bear. Behind him I can see a painting of a girl sailing. He's a gentle man, sometimes he puts his pen in his mouth and it disappears into his facial hair. He doesn't breathe, then he takes a big long breath that raises his trunk and shoulders. He pays attention to detail. I don't have to keep reminding him who my sister is when I mention her name.

"You keep a lot to yourself, don't you."

Deep breath.

"I don't lose my keys anymore because I don't have keys. I don't crash into things because I can't drive. I'm not fighting with my parents because they're not here. I'm not buying mushrooms because you won't let me leave. I'm not skipping class or sleeping in school because I'm not in school. I'm not forgetting things because I've got nothing to remember. So what do you think?"

Pins and needles in my eyes; I shouldn't let myself yell.

When I get emotional he writes it down on his yellow pad.

"I think you're a smart young woman with a future," he said. "I think you're doing your best to get through this."

No, I thought.

We looked at each other, I heard another office door close.

"What do you want, more than anything else?"

"To stay up all night," I said instantly.

I was thinking of Lennie. He wakes me. Going away together maybe.

Then I yawned.

He wrote some more.

"Sometimes people just yawn, you know."

He grinned.

"We're going to have to stop there," he said.

I shrugged.

The other narcoleptics (like when I used to go to camp):

Karryn, Australian, schoolteacher.

Dim, paper merchant. Jet black hair.

Helder: was born in Lebanon. Guileless.

Serena: music journalist.

I take pills from my boot-shaped locket.

You never call a ventriloquist's dummy a dummy. They don't like that; they have names. The word ventriloquism comes from the Latin for speaking and belly. Lennie also does magic, and once he performed for Elton John.

We were lying in the long yellow grass off one of the paths. Low behind three maples. People walking by could barely see us, only if they looked. But we could hear them come and go. I felt the warmth rising in me as my skin met his, and the deeper we kissed the less I could feel it: I felt something bubbling inside me and I pulled away. I didn't want to stop. To have to stop made me angry. Then I had to calm down from that too.

"My darling duck," said Lennie, and I kissed him on the arm, breathed.

Then pulled away, out of contact, for the best.

Lennie's the opposite of me.

He said he was doing the study for the money. Dr. Frink had been pestering him for years. He did something with his eyebrows that gave him Dr. Frink's caring bewildered eager gaze. His condition was unique. The study was funded by NASA. The U.S. army was curious too, but Lennie wasn't so into that. He's like some kind of Norwegian, he said: he's awake half the year. Then he sleeps for six months at a time.

"You're more fucked up than I am!" I said, delighted.

He pretended to pout and I kissed his dark green T-shirt sleeve.

"I haven't seen winter in eight years," Lennie said like a plantation owner. "That's why you know I've got such a great tan." He does these voices . . .

No work or school to keep us from each other.

Sex is one of my triggers. It does a little too much to me. At least it did: halfway through my one sexual experience, I disappeared. First I couldn't move my left side, and then suddenly I was laughing and I couldn't stop, and the poor boy I was with took it very very badly. "It's not you," I kept saying, coughing and shaking, laughing, wrapping the sheet around me, "it's not you," and soon he was in tears.

We kissed. I stayed longer than I should have. Earth under my jeans, grass against my back, his scratchy face. I drew away and gasped.

"Sorry," said Lennie. He stroked my cheek with soft knuckles.

On the path two insomniacs walked by with tennis rackets.

"What's it like?"

"Normal for four five months. Then close to when I go under—I feel it coming—I start to get pretty manic. The way I understand it is it's like I need a break from the world? I start making calls, crazy phone calls, to Steven Spielberg because he should make a movie about me, to the TONY awards, Where's my statuette. I'm learning Italian, I'm writing letters to the *Times*, I'm laughing constantly, okay? I write and rehearse a show in three days and I think it's the best work ever done by man or woman. Spending a lot of time on the subway writing down the numbers of the cars. There's a letter in my back pocket telling people what to do if they find me. Dr. Frink's PalmPilot beeps and he gives me a call, begs me to come in. I start to see this orange glow around the edge of things, the smell of mint. I'm angry. Don't feel like myself anymore, my eyes are burning and scratching, not feeling like anything any more. Then boom, in a cab, in the shower, backstage, boom, I'm out. Eventually someone finds me and they take me to hospital and eventually they figure things out and they bring me here, okay? Nice Asian nurses. But it's close now, I'm close to going under. This is the first year I haven't been all crazy."

He reached his arm around me and kissed my head. Our limbs together like putting bikes away in the garage.

"How close?"

"Next week, sweetcheeks."

Me floating in amber.

Then, up on my elbows:

"I always tell people I fight it," I said. "Struggling to stay awake like struggling to stay afloat and I fight it, I spit water out of my mouth. It's true."

I swallowed and looked at how he was looking at me, inches away. "But you know, there's a pleasure in giving up. There's a pleasure in going under. Knowing everything's lost. Sometimes there's a part of you that just wants to give up."

I never told anyone before.

"I'll be dreaming of you the whole time I'm out, baby," he said.

I looked at him with big wet eyes: he burst out laughing at me.

"You son of a bitch," I said, and I slapped him. And then we were wrestling and laughing.

• • •

Before coming here my school sent me to see my GP because I'd got anxious and fainted in a geology exam on question 4 ("Describe the situation of three sedimentary rocks") and they couldn't wake me and they'd carried me out of the gym. (I failed.) My GP didn't know what to do with me and he sent me to a neurologist. Then I went back to see my GP, and he sent me to a psychiatrist. All these doctors. It didn't work, and I went to see a Chinese naturopath. He gave me some twigs and bark that were ridged and brown like his own skin. I boiled them into a tea that stank up the entire house. I went back to see my GP. He didn't know what to do with me. I was out of school by now. Near my parents there was a community centre, a support group: women in a circle talking about their symptoms as if their symptoms were their children. *My symptoms are developing so quickly—Guess what my symptoms did this week!* Me too. I remember bits and pieces, without them adding up into anything. I was better off in chatrooms, heard a lot about various meds. I spent a lot of time online: no whiny voices. Someone mentioned the clinic. And so.

1. Will you remember me when you wake up?
2. Was it just fun for you?
3. What are you thinking about?
4. Will you wake up even?
5. What did you mean when you said you thought consciousness was overrated?
6. Will we go on the road together or was that just play?
7. Do you understand me, really?

8. What do your parents do? I forgot to ask.
9. Can I buy you a new Cuban shirt?
10. You look like a punk Cary Grant.
11. Are you dreaming of me?
12. I can't wait any longer.

In my dream Lennie was telling me he'd slept with someone else and I was telling him it was OK. Then he had to give a lecture on the spread of plastics after the war (there was a documentary about it) and I was helping him prepare in the big empty theatre. But then I was a waitress and he had gone. I woke up and I knew it was my room because of the three lines the light makes on the ceiling coming through the blinds. I wanted to get up, then I wanted to call for help. But I could not move.

I started hoarding my meds.

Then every day I cried for the whole fifty minutes with Dr. Frink. He looked worried and he passed me the box of tissues and I cried. I didn't want to talk about anything. I was crying into one hand the way I always did.

"Do you see how you're sitting?"

I cried.

"You're holding on to the chair arm. In case you black out, isn't it?"

I cried more.

Dr. Frink started talking about chaos. He said, "Complex systems can flip from one mode to another. When inputs grow too great, the system jumps from one equilibrium to a different one. Something like this happens to your friend."

I kept crying. Lennie's spiky thick black hair.

"It may be something similar happens to you," he said. "When your inputs become too much to deal with . . . you shut down. I know it doesn't feel good but do you see it's good that you're crying, talking?"

"I don't want to cry," I said into Kleenex. "I don't want to be here. I don't want to talk."

He looked gently at me, waiting.

Blackouts: 4

These moments of lucidity I can't build into anything.

Night-time. But I was not sleeping. Like I said, I've been hoarding my meds. I felt tired as a mermaid dredged up from the bottom of the sea.

A change of clothes, a toothbrush, Dr. Frink's Visa card from the top right-hand drawer of his desk.

Sid the night nurse sleeps in front of his monitors and I walk by cool as techno. The wheelchair runs silently on the blue carpet.

You looked different. They'd shaved your head and wired you up. Your shoulders were slack and there was nothing holding together your muscles. The room was full of machines. The two grey hairs sticking out from your undershirt almost made me cry. I kissed you but you didn't wake up.

Pulling the tape off his skin to release the gummy electrodes hurt *me*. I kissed each spot after doing it. He swallowed. I pulled the blue sheet away. He was wearing boxers, and long white gym socks with a red border. I brought the wheelchair close to the bed and pushed it away again, because it was in the way. I stood at the end of the bed and grabbed Lennie's two shins and pulled his legs to the left but he didn't help me out—his top half was still.

"Don't you want to get out of here?"

Problem-solving is the opposite of automatic behaviour.

From the other side of the bed I tried to push him onto his side. There was a pillow. I bunched it under his back so he wouldn't slide down. It didn't work. It struck me: moving an unwilling man around is one of the hardest things you can do.

Suddenly I was exhausted. My head dropped but my neck snapped up and woke me. Moving to the other side of the bed I pulled Lennie's knees up and slid them towards me, then tugged the wheelchair closer with my foot and tried to slide him into it sideways. Gradually his feet and calves came off the bed but I was in the way. I moved round him again and pulled again, but he was too heavy, and he came off the bed and fell on to me and we knocked the wheelchair back into the dresser. I was under him, bruised. I was wrapped up under Lennie in just his underwear. He smelled like soap; they'd been looking after him. I saw then, under the bed, a white crank with black handle, a tool for raising and lowering the bed, and I kicked at it.

I don't think too long passed. I woke. My toe hurt. Sliding out from under Lennie I pulled the wheelchair to us, put the brake on this time, and with my legs wide apart lifted him up into sitting. I stood there breathing heavily, sweat on my neck. Wheeling him down the hall I didn't run into anyone.

We took an ambulance from the hospital garage.

At the strip mall I bought sunglasses and lunch meats. If there'd been a medical supply store I could have bought Lennie a new IV, but I wouldn't know what to put in it.

We slept in the parking lot. In each other's arms. I figured they'd be looking for us at the airports and seaports. They have so many ambulances I thought they wouldn't miss one. It was cold but it was a blissful night. I told him that in the morning we'd start for Mexico. I just needed to rest my eyes for a minute.

Sirens woke me, stringy and jumpy and completely exhausted.

Police cars filed into the parking lot in a chain and horseshoed themselves around us. Followed by fire-trucks and other ambulances. The policemen opened their doors and kneeled to aim guns at us. I could see the lake behind them.

"Well, Lennie," I said.

"Sweetheart, I love you for what you've done," said Lennie.

He looked pretty radiant in the black seat next to me, mouth open, sunglasses all askew aimed at the sky, spit crawling down his cheek. I wiped that off on my sleeve.

"Now we'll never be apart," Lennie said.

His voice came out too high, I did it again.

"Now we'll never be apart," Lennie said.

"Lennie," I sighed, "You sound just like Elvis."

"I crack me up," he said in my voice.

I was laughing.

I rolled down the window and stuck my head out.

"What do you want?" I yelled.

No one answered.

A blue Oldsmobile drew up behind the police and out came Dr. Frink. He looked bedraggled and nervous, in wide jeans and a sweater, and when he came to stand next to the bulky black vests of the policemen he looked as light and thin as a locust. One of them leaned into him urgently. Dr. Frink put his hands up in a *No no no* kind of way.

In the middle between us there was a control panel with square buttons the size of chunks of chocolate. There were piles of yellow forms and white forms tied with elastic bands and two clipboards, and a box of white gloves. I put a pair on.

Dr. Frink lifted a blue-and-white loudspeaker to his mouth. The policeman next to him waved three fingers at one of his subordinates. It took Dr. Frink a minute to figure out the buttons. Then, "Hi Lena," came his bass voice, amplified and fuzzy.

I picked up the radio thing and pushed a red button and a yellow one until I heard my voice bounce out above me.

"Dr. Frink," I said. "You look good. You shouldn't always wear a suit to work."

"Thanks, Lena . . . We need to check how Lennie's doing."

"Can you get me some smokes?" I said.

He turned to the policeman next to him, who shook his head.

"You're putting Lennie in danger, Lena. Come out now."

"I took your Visa card. Sorry."

"That's okay, Lena."

"How'd you find us?"

Dr. Frink looked at the policeman again. This time he shrugged.

"There are security cameras all over the clinic. You stole an ambulance. You don't know how to drive."

"I can drive!" I yelled.

I leaned over and pulled Lennie up with me and gave him the CB. "I'm okay," he said. "I'm perfectly happy. Please, all of you, go home."

Dr. Frink dropped the conch to his hip. The tall cop looked at him.

"Let's just talk, Lena."

"Lena's fine too," Lennie said, still eyes closed staring up at the sky. "She's fine. You know, you should just leave us alone. We're in love."

The cop had a loudspeaker too.

"Young lady, you're in a lot of trouble. The best thing you can do for your friend is put down the mike, open the door, and come out of the ambulance with your hands in the air."

"You'll never take us alive!" I yelled.

The cops by the nearest car smiled at each other. I'd put the fear of god into them.

Behind the circle of police cars I could see two paramedics in orange clothes chatting beside their ambulance, one of them leaning back against it. They looked relaxed. The lake was like the perfect top of a skipping stone. There was mist, and a low white ball: the sun. I wanted Lennie to be able to see it too so I lowered his window and pushed him with my feet so his head was poking out of the window.

"Beautiful," he said. I pulled him back in. I didn't want them to shoot him or anything.

My breathing was shallow and hurried, and his breaths were long and calm, as if he'd done this a hundred times. I wondered what it would be like to drive into the lake and be submerged together.

"What do you think, Lennie?"

He was still.

"I think it's time to give up, Lena."

I leaned over to kiss him and the stupid awkward dispatching computer dug into my side, and I knocked over an old coffee cup. I opened up his mouth and dabbed away the dry spit. He tasted like him. We kissed for a long time. He was breathing deeply into me now. We kissed and I lifted his tongue and I licked all around and under it and it was almost powdery as we kissed. I felt the thing sweeping up from inside me but I didn't want to stop now; I wanted to be where he was.

I felt tears coming on, and under my closed eyes everything was black and orange. I didn't let go or pull back, I thought perhaps he was waking but no, no. His new stubble felt rough against my cheeks, I put my hand inside the jean jacket, my jean jacket he was wearing and felt the warmth of his chest and his heart beating inside. It all turned white as I fell again and there was nothing to scrabble against or hold onto and that was all.

When I woke up my hand was in his.

No one's going to press charges.

NIP IT IN THE BUD

"Can you do my back, sweetie?" she said remembering. She lay chest down on the lime green towel and knotted her arms behind her, like a wooden doll, to unclip her black bikini top.

It was the hottest day of the summer. Some days the lake was scratched with diamonds like snakeskin; today it was a sizzling black bowl. And two steps on the sand burned feet. It was August and as usual there was no one visible all the way down the beach. Strewn around they had magazines and bottled water and sunglasses and an unused Frisbee and her Discman and the iPod she'd just bought him. They were rich. It was a far drive from the city.

"Sweetie?" she said. Sighing he put down his book face open and looked at her, irritated. From his chair in the hot shade of the parasol he reached down for the squat beige cylinder. It was warm to the touch. He scooped out thick wet white cream and kneeled on the towel next to her, shin against *People* magazine and flip-flops. He rubbed his hands together.

Smelling coconut he massaged the cream into her shoulders and the spotty triangle between them. She was bony and familiar. Each time her skin reminded him of chicken thighs: damp and giving, with blotches of red and blue. He could pierce it with a steak knife and pull it all away and there would be the purple flesh below. He closed his eyes not to see, not to feel her peeling skin on his fingers.

"Hmmm," she sighed.

He reached back for more cream and felt the sand hot on his kneecap and wiped sweat off his forehead. Polishing her back he couldn't but look: beauty spots glistening under the cream. Some of it had disappeared into the skin to make it shine and some of it remained in lines like cake mix in a licked bowl. And the withered cup of one breast shapeless on the towel. He suppressed a shudder and closed his eyes again. She made him do this four times a day.

"That's lovely," she said, enjoying the touch of his small hands. "Thank you."

When he was done and was quickly reading again she rolled up onto her side and unconcerned asked "Do you want me to do you?" and he shook his head making sure not to see her. *It is not for Faust's sake that I shall dwell further on this point,* he read. With one arm to her chest she swaddled her breasts as if she were carrying eggs and looked around for her top and then facing the lake replaced it. She lay in the sun and he read.

"Well I'm going to see about lunch," she yawned into her magazine later.

"Okay mom," he said, still reading.

With a turquoise wrap over her shoulders and top Jackie Austyn walked up the path through sandy reeds to the cottage.

On her mind was something her son had said. A month before she'd got him to come with her on a walk up the beach in the afternoon. She'd pestered him a little—he was moody all the time now, it was his age—and finally he'd opened his mouth. He told her about the book he was reading and of course it had all gone way over her head but one thing he'd said explaining it stuck: *Well everyone has this feeling they'd rather be someone else, don't they?*

"I don't," she'd replied immediately, worried for him. "I never wanted to be anyone else. Why? I wouldn't be happier."

She was passing the creek now but thinking, not looking around at where she was. A breeze made her pull the light cloth closer round herself.

She almost wished he were more like other teenagers drinking and smoking. She wished he had friends here. He hates me now, she thought, and was shocked to feel tears starting hot above behind her nose as she thought of them cocooned together in all the summers there, swimming, together, playing Monopoly if it rained. Always just the two of them.

Her husband Leo Austyn had died when Eddie was still just a baby. But Leo was twenty-five years older than her and she'd known instantly though not without guilt that his heart attack had spared her decades of boredom. Her brothers-in-law, partners at the company which bore what shortly before had become her surname, gave her some trouble at the death but really the will was straightforward: he had left his wife and son everything. Fifteen years passed and they invited her and Eddie for Christmas and Thanksgiving and sent him cheques for his birthday and that was all. She had not looked for another man, though she'd had offers, nor had she worked. She had dedicated herself to her son.

Once you crested the dunes you could see the dark green triangle of the cottage. The reeds gave way to a stone path and the lawn of her garden and two picnic tables and a third under a tree where she went for secret smokes. Beyond them gently further uphill was the hot tub on the great sun deck you could see the lake from. Inside, the main floor was one big room with a dining table and an imposing stone fireplace which they never used because they never came up in winter. There was a gallery upstairs with their bedrooms and rooms she called the study and the guest bedroom and so forth; Leo had built the cottage for his entire family to enjoy so for years now several rooms stayed empty. The basement was finished also and next to the furnace room and storage for all Eddie's old tiny surfboards and beach balls there was a pool table sleeping unused under layers of dust. She'd bought it for Eddie but he never went down there. When she came up to the house on Sundays Mary Jackson from the town sometimes ran a cloth over the oilskin on top of it. Mary cleaned and in the winter she kept an eye on the pipes and made sure everything with the house was okay. She'd had a cancer scare earlier in the summer that had kept her from coming for six weeks. She was a widow also.

"Well I don't know why you're even talking about the States. U of T is a good school. Trinity."

He said nothing.

"Well why?"

"Mom I just want to keep my options open okay?"

"Of course. I want you to keep your options open. All I'm saying is U of T is a good school. That's all."

"I know it's a good school."

"You're a year younger than everyone else already."

"Year and a half," he said.

He'd complained before about her 'hectoring' him so she said no more. But she didn't want him to leave.

"Maybe we should turn the AC up," she said, making her voice light. "It's too warm in here."

She didn't like to prepare food unless the air was cool and sterile. For cooking she put a silk cloth around her head like a turban and though she was unpeeling slices of processed cheese it made her feel like a French film star. Laid out in front of her all together she had white bread and mustard and mayonnaise and turkey and tomato with all the juicy seeds spilling out onto the counter. She cut the crusts off his bread.

"We could eat down on the beach," she suggested.

Holding the knife she turned to look at him. His hair was straight and short and always looked wet; Leo had had curly thick hair. He looked thin and diffident to her, elbows on the island in the middle of the kitchen, white t-shirt and green swimming trunks. Waiting to be fed, moody and hungry like a hatchling. She thought he should do more sports and she'd said it a hundred times. She opened her mouth to say it again: *You have the whole summer the lake and all you do is read* but thought better and said nothing.

"What?" he said, provoked.

"Nothing. I said we could eat lunch down on the beach that's all."

It was hot by the fridge. She turned back to the counter and squeezed mayonnaise out. There were other kids up here, she sometimes saw them on sailboats and jet-skis but he never swam out and said hi. There were even kids from the town he could get to meet if he wanted. And his schoolfriends? Did he have any?

"Mrs. Franklin used to say—"

"I know Mom—"

"Well she used to say even in grade three how smart you were. You could do all your sums and tell time and she had to give you more work because you were done before any of the other kids. She said Look out for him he's a smart one. And at night you always wanted me to read you another story, another story, just one more mommy . . ."

She smiled at the thick tomato slices and then felt by his silence that he wasn't in the room any more. Half turning over her shoulder she looked for him. He had gone to the coffee table and had the remote control and she heard the ploongk of the television and satellite starting up.

"Oh sweetie," she said loud, "Can you drive down to the store for me this afternoon? I made a list."

Coming towards her remote in hand, motorbikes on the television behind him, he said, "Sure."

Cherry-faced.

She wiped her hands and puzzled she pulled the list out from under the plumber's magnetic card on the fridge to give to him. His Adam's apple rose up.

"Sure," he said.

For a big shop they drove into town. But for the goods on his list in her wild pencil—milk, pancake mix, something like *joyug* he couldn't make out—there was Peter's Convenience at the intersection with six on the edge of Renforth. It was a peeling white rectangle with two aisles of cereal and bread and popcorn and peanut butter, a low fridge with cheese and milk, candies at the front and a wall of movies half of which were new and half of which were mysterious, from the 80s. Usually there were children running in and out buying ice cream but today it was too hot and the entrance door was open. Outside the intersection was still.

She was leaning with a ballpoint over a textbook and he tried not to stare as he walked up and down the short aisles pulling down warm canned pasta sauce and potato chips and with them dust. He knew where everything in the store was as well as she did by now and yet they had never said any more to each other than hey and see ya. Sometimes they spoke about it being hot or the rain if it had rained though it hadn't rained in weeks; so he couldn't talk about that. Unless he said *It hasn't rained.*

If she looks up now she loves me, he repeated to himself silently, looking at Tropicana. He looked hard at sell-by dates, listened to the soft rock. There was nothing he could ask about. He breathed in deeply to relax but silently so it wouldn't be obvious he was trying to relax. She was writing something into her book. There was a fan above her and when it blew in her direction the pages rustled. There were no newspapers left. He looked at the sun hats.

At the counter it was cooler.

The total came to $7.27.

"I've only got a fifty."

"No problem," she smiled.

She beeped the register and he closed his mouth and she gave him his change and he slid it into the small pocket inside the top of his shorts. She was wearing her red retro Hot Wheels t-shirt. It covered up a pendant on a black string around her neck; he could see the shape of it below the red fabric. Her neck. She moved his mom's things into a plastic bag for him and he thought he should have offered to do that for her.

"Pretty hot this week, huh?"

"Record temperatures," she said.

And then he had to think of something else to say.

He gestured at the counter.

"Are you studying?"

"French," she said, then asked with her eyes, holding up the eggs, if she should put them in a different bag. "For summer school."

"What grade are you in?"

"Eleven."

"Twelve."

"Yeah where?"

He hesitated. He didn't want to sound like he was full of himself or trying to impress her or put her down.

"In the city."

She pushed the bags across the counter to him and so he had something to do with his hands.

"I've already been through the book twice and I'm getting nowhere. I hate it. I've written all the answers in already. But I want to go to Quebec on exchange next year?"

Holding the white bags he felt that was the signal to leave. But as in a film he saw what he was about to say next before he said it: the sentence entered his head fully formed like an ad. He saw it above him. But still surprised himself when he heard himself say it.

"I have some French books you could borrow."

He felt sweat. He waited for someone to come in and take her attention away.

"I mean it probably wouldn't be that useful because they're pretty old and everything but if you wanted . . . it would be something else you could be reading, I guess."

"No, this book is like . . . that would be great. Thank you."

She said it so naturally.

"I could bring them down," he said excited.

"You don't have to do that. I'll pick them up. You're up off seventeen?"

"No I'll bring them down—"

"Oh I don't want you to go to—"

"No, it's okay. I like to drive in."

She smiled and said thanks again and he felt the glow start in his feet and work its way up. She hadn't said no. He scraped his elbow on the counter on his way out then stopped.

"Eddie," he said.

"Oh, I know. I'm Patti."

Wanting to laugh he told himself it wasn't a big deal to her, just a nice thing a neighbour was doing, nothing more than that. But he had never been able to do it before. Unlocking the car he knew he'd be replaying this conversation the entire drive home, and that when he was talking to his mother over dinner and watching

TV that night and reading he'd hear her soft natural *thank you* again and again. He was so jittery driving back that he had to stop the car twice and remind himself to slow down. On the side of the road he yelled at the trees.

"You tan so naturally Patti my skin just puckers."

Patti laughed not knowing what to say.

"Are you part native?"

"No," said Patti, surprised. "I don't think so."

"No, you do. What's your secret my darling?" Jackie asked. "How do you keep so thin? Don't tell me—you're a low carb girl, aren't you?"

She began to answer that she did yoga sometimes but Jackie kept talking.

"No of course you're not there's no secret. You're just young that's all, you make me feel so old and horrible like a great beached whale. Sit up straight Eddie would you it's terrible for your back sweetie."

He fixed his posture and they all three sat up more erect, even Patti and Jackie on the soft brown leather of the ancient couch.

"You look like Angeline Jolie," Jackie was saying. "But blonde. Blonde and tanned, look at you. You're lucky."

"No one ever said I looked like her before," answered Patti, happy.

Now Jackie was exuberantly surprised.

"Really? No? But I think she's a tremendous actress. Did you see *Crossing Borders*? Doesn't she look like Angeline Jolie, Eddie? But blonde."

"Angelina," Eddie said.

Patti was surprised by how much Eddie's mom was talking to her. It was weird anyway though; she wasn't used to hanging out

with people's parents. Usually if she was hanging out at someone's house the parents were out, or upstairs.

She and Jackie sat together on the couch and Eddie was quiet
on a stiff black wooden chair on the other side of the coffee table
and he looked like he was sulking. Jackie swivelled extravagantly
to speak to him but mostly tucked in to Patti. They each had a
glass of white wine; Patti had asked for a beer but they had none.
Jackie seemed excited to have her there; Eddie was looking hard
at each stone of the fireplace, one after another.

"He hasn't been to the movies in months so what does he
know anyway," Jackie said. "There's a perfectly good cinema in
Hawksville but he never wants to go."

An idea came to her.

"We could go all together."

"Mom," Eddie said finally, flat, leaning forward towards her.

"We have movies at the store," Patti said.

"He won't go to the movies but he spends the whole summer
reading."

She saw his face and said quick to Patti, "I'm embarrassing
him."

She rolled her eyes.

"Whatever I do I'm embarrassing him. Do you criticize your
mother, Patti?"

"Well," she hesitated, inches from Jackie's squeezed anxious
features.

"I knew it. My god, you have such a lovely smile. Eddie she's
so gorgeous!"

Patti blushed, confused. Jackie was staring at her and it made
her uncomfortable.

She was used to driving out to the quarry to drink with
friends from school and smoking and hanging out with Annie.

"Look at that!"

Jackie sighed, hand across her chest, eyes crossed racing up to the ceiling.

"Tell me how your Aunt Mary's doing Patti," said Jackie with great sincere concern.

Forty-five minutes before, Patti had closed the door to her mother's hatchback and pulled up her sweatpants over her tattoo, feeling her feet sink into wide round stones. She walked up to the house in half-light though the sky was still bright.

Driving to her friend Annie's she had thought *I can just stop in pick them up* and she was curious about the house; her Aunt Mary had said it was total luxury. Yes Eddie was scrawny and maybe he had a bit of a thing for her, but at least he didn't have the beer-can-crushed-against-forehead meatball bullshit of her friends or the rich boys up here in the summer they sometimes picked fights with. Many times in the store because she was cute and slender she'd been invited up to a party in one of the big houses, by some white-beige-chino-shorts-wearing-wristbanded asshole in Oakleys buying mix. They made fires on the beach and drank coolers and talked about clubs in the city she'd never heard of. Someone always had a guitar. Eventually they paired off and walked into the dunes together, each rich tanned boy with a poor girl in his hand. She hated it.

She'd rung the bell and waited. Mrs. A had come to the door looking vamped up the way Aunt Mary always described her: like an old-time actress, with lots of rings and a thick silver band hanging from her neck. She'd stood there just looking at Patti.

"Mrs. Austyn? I'm here to see Eddie?" Patti said. "He has some books for me?"

Without smiling or turning her head Mrs. A had called out of the side of her mouth.

"Edward! There's a young lady here to see you. Call me Jackie, please."

She'd laughed but then looked at Patti suspicious.

"What books is he giving you?"

"Some French books? He said he'd drop them off but I was driving by and I thought . . ."

Edward had been standing behind his mother by now, and Patti had waved hi and he hadn't responded. He'd looked scared.

"You're not Mary Jackson's girl are you?" Mrs. A had said.

"Yeah. That's my aunt."

"I thought so." Finally Mrs. A, Jackie, had smiled, without warmth, and automatically Patti had smiled back. "She does the house, you know. Well come in my darling."

"I can't really," she said, but Mrs. A insisted, and almost pulled her over the threshold. Outside it was humid and clingy but inside the house the air was freezing.

"Well fetch her books, Edward. What can I get you to drink?"

Eddie brought down an extra black chair from upstairs because there were only two at the table. It gave Patti the feeling that by being there she was making everything in the house different. She hadn't wanted to stay especially and had felt immediately uncomfortable but Jackie had insisted with a kind of urgent necessity that there was enough food, she was cooking already, and Patti hadn't been able to say no enough times and here she was as if in a dream. She'd heard Eddie's loud whispers from the kitchen and made sure her cell was on and sipped wine, looking round at all the space and the wood and wondering what a television that size cost.

Jackie hadn't let her help in the kitchen and there were some awkward silent minutes on the couch where she thought Eddie wanted her to leave and they said nothing to each other and he wiped his forehead and even seemed to shake a little and their breathing was interrupted by Jackie humming in the kitchen and shouting out questions.

Then Jackie stood at the corner of the wooden table with her hands extended by salad tongs deep into the purple bowl. She pushed her thigh into the table edge. Her place was at the head of the table and Patti sat facing Eddie's empty dead face; he didn't look up at her from his plate much and she felt sorry for him and wanted to go.

Jackie mixed the salad and poured store-bought dressing freely over it.

"Do you want everything together Patti or salad first?" she asked.

"Together, please."

Jackie grinned.

"You need to put some skin on your bones dear you're skin and bone."

Again Eddie briefly hid his face in his hands as if wiping it.

"I didn't have a thing in the fridge Patti but Eddie didn't give me any warning so we'll just have to lump it."

"Oh no I shouldn't just have—"

Usually when Patti ate it was her at the kitchen counter watching TV, her parents still at work. She liked to eat early then go out.

The salad was spinach leaves and cubed feta. Jackie served herbed chicken from a low white rectangular tray with roses painted on. Then she asked Eddie for his plate and spooned on new potatoes.

"I'll give you a leg it's his favourite. When he was a boy Patti all he would eat is drumsticks."

"No, no peas," he said.

"But you always have peas."

She piled them up on to the chicken.

Patti followed his eyes to see what he was looking at outside but to her the windows were completely dark. She was surprised because she would have expected to see Crawson Point or the lights from some of the cottages across the lake or a boat out but there was nothing; they didn't even have lights on going down the path. But he stared in that direction at the uninhabited black fabric.

Patti looked back down and saw that Jackie was cutting Edward's food up. First she thought Mrs. A had got confused about whose plate was whose. She wanted to say something but nothing came. Jackie was pulling the skin away for him and shearing tender flesh from the bone. She had sliced half of the meat when she stopped and looked up at him, mouth hanging slightly open like a child amazed to have been caught in a lie. She bit her lip.

"Mom," said Eddie and pulled his plate from her clanging it dully against the tray of peas.

Jackie covered her mouth embarrassed but then she looked down at Patti and couldn't suppress a laugh, and then the two of them giggled together and snorted and Patti wanted to stop for Eddie's sake but really it was funny.

"Oh dear, dear," Jackie said between giggles. "Oh I'm sorry sweetie. Oh dear."

She kissed him on the head; he froze.

She sighed still laughing.

"Give Mommy some more wine dear."

"Yeah I don't think you need any more," he said, hard-voiced and resentful.

"Really Edward don't be so silly. It was just a mistake. Once a mother, Patti."

She reached for the wine herself.

"I'm laughing at me, not at you. You needn't be embarrassed."

Patti looked at Eddie and then she quickly looked away like touching a white coal; wet lines blurred the Us of his eyes

Jackie went to fetch salt and pepper and Edward turned to Patti his cheeks red and she felt he was surely about to say something. She cringed inside and he waited and opened his mouth but he didn't speak, looking at her instead. A clatter from the kitchen made him speak.

"She sneaks into my bed," said Edward. "Tonight. She won't even let me sleep by myself."

Patti pretended not to hear.

His mother came gaily back in.

"You'll see when you have kids of your own," Jackie said, and sitting down leaned so close in that her features swooped and stretched into garish shapes.

Edward was taking dishes into the kitchen. Jackie wouldn't let Patti help. They sat talking, Jackie's hand on Patti's forearm, holding her in place.

"I feel I can really talk to you Patti. You know," she said in quiet confidential tone, "He's very shy. Leo was never like that nor am I so I don't understand it. He doesn't ever have friends over."

He appeared at the table again and picked up glasses.

"Not yet!" Jackie shrieked.

"Okay, okay."

He put serving tongs in the empty salad bowl and took that with him.

"I feel like I know you already. You're a simple soul, I don't meet people like you in the city. And he's not very what's the word gregarious. When you have children: it's the most wonderful thing in the world! But your life belongs to someone else."

Suddenly her face clouded but Jackie wasn't sure if it was emotion or fake drunken sentimentality.

"After Leo died I had, you know, offers of course but I just couldn't, not with *him*. But I don't know, did I do the right thing? I have needs too, you know."

Patti didn't know where to look.

She saw that Eddie was standing above her and was silent.

"Why don't you offer Patti some coffee darling?"

When he had gone again—napkins chicken skin and cutlery piled on plates—she whispered to invite complicity.

"For a long time he was the most terrible bedwetter. He *still* has trouble sleeping by himself. Scared of the dark!"

When Patti left tipsy and astounded she forgot the French books on the bamboo bench by the front door. At her car she heard Jackie clunk down the steps towards her, and was hugged too close goodbye again and smelled strong perfume again. She could see Eddie watching them from the doorway, backlit.

On a Saturday the next summer Patti was on the eastern side of the lake. Out in the water she imagined she could see all the way across to the other side: she imagined the dark green triangle of the big house and two stick figures lying next to each other on the beach. But it was so bright that it hurt her eyes to keep staring out.

"What are you dreaming about gorgeous?" said Brad beneath her and lightly drily they kissed.

Then pushing the yellow float they swam back to their friends.

THE MILE HIGH CLUB

Clark tried the door again, but it was as intransigent as matter. He rattled the silver knob, but it was stuck. He tried the door again, and then rattled the silver knob again, but he was stuck. The toilet was not a pleasant place to be. The stench coming from the U-bend was disgusting (though he could at least recognize in it his own sweet contribution), there was urine spattered toilet paper strewn around the floor, and in black ink on the door graffiti of terrifying anatomical marvels. There was very little space for him—the train might be a mile long, but he was trapped in a tiny portion of it.

He decided to sit down again. He wanted to wipe the lid first, but there wasn't one, so he took a napkin from the mouth at thigh-height, pushed the long rectangular lever for cold water, and wiped the seat. (I know, I know, it sounds like an airplane toilet, but believe me, all this happens on a plane. Train. All this happens on a train. A mile long.) He scrumpled the napkin and dropped it in the bin, and sat himself down in the usual way, bent at the knees, the customary position, but with his trousers on, awaiting his fate. It was not a promising place to be. He tried not to breathe in through his nose, shaken from side to side by the turbulence. Of the tracks. Rattling the train.

Clark was trapped in his own thoughts. He was on his way to see his fiancée, the lovely Darla, and oh the locked-away secret he had to tell her. There was a part of him that wanted to tell her nothing. That had always worked in the past. But another part of him suspected that if this first part of him had its way, the secret would darkly metastasize, and soon their entire relationship would be rotted through. Like wood. Or at least his part of their relationship would be. It was sometimes hard for Clark to be honest with the lovely Darla, she was a much better person than he was. Which is why he was always screwing around.

Of course, there was another part of Clark—he was an unnecessarily complex person—which thought that he'd committed the sin of adultery with all those stewardesses simply in order to be free of the lovely Darla, though he loved her still. And another part of him which argued that the fact of the adultery he had committed demonstrated that he was already free, and just hadn't got round to telling her yet. All this is the psychological bit. He was mulling it all over, not in these words.

It struck him that the perfect resolution would be the lovely Darla + stewardesses, but even Clark knew that the lovely Darla was unlikely to bite at that particular plum.

Either way, he was stuck in the bog with no way out. That was the immediate difficulty.

Clark tried the door again, but it was as intransigent as matter. He rattled the silver knob, but it was stuck. He tried the door again, and then rattled the silver knob again, but he was stuck. The toilet was not a pleasant place to be. The stench coming from the U-bend was disgusting (though he could at least recognize in it his own sweet contribution), there was urine spattered toilet paper strewn around the floor, and in black ink on the door graffiti of terrifying anatomical marvels. There was very little space for him—the train might be a mile long, but he was trapped in a tiny portion of it.

Just then, the train stopped. Not suddenly. I should have said, it had been meandering along at a very slow rate, like an airliner in a holding pattern in a huge rectangle around Gatwick, seeming to move more from side to side than forward, as happens on parts of the track that are under repair or just dilapidated, that is, out of date. There was a shudder and then they were still. The lights flic-flacked. The chudge-ajug chudge-ajug was replaced by an electronic whine. Surely someone will be able to hear me now, thought Clark, but not in words.

They were still still. He stood up and pounded with both hands on the grey plastic door calling out, "Help me! Help me! Help me!" His voice bounced around him but of course no one came. Pausing, he thought: Serves me right for using a public toilet, I should have held it in. (If it had been an airplane toilet, he could have pushed the call button and in forty minutes a tousle-haired stewardess would have come. But he was in a train!) He tried the door again, and then rattled the silver knob again, but he was stuck. Well, he was no philosopher: he hit and kicked the door until sweating, he grew tired, his body I mean, and he sat down, on the bog.

He stood up. He tried the door again, but it was, you know. There were no windows, he could not see the landscape not rushing by, he couldn't see the beauty of nature, he lifted the toilet lid, freshly cleaned. At the base of the bowl there was a metal panel. He flushed—not his skin tone, he flushed the toilet—and the panel opened, and he could see pebbles and iron beneath him. The earth. Natural light, or at least natural shadow. He was only this far away from freedom, but short of transforming himself into a poo, he didn't know how to take advantage. He wiped the seat and sat down again.

This is neurosis, he thought. I sit down, I stand up, I pound the door, my mind is racing. I go from door to bog and bog to door—two paces—I get nothing done, my hair is falling out. Of all the places to punish me, you absolute cock. Though of course he didn't believe in such notions as the Creator, let alone neurosis. Feeling dramatic he shook his fist at the ceiling, which is curious because it's not a gesture you see so many people make these days: it's out of date.

Just then, he remembered a deus ex machina, a cellphone, in his pocket. He settled down to breaking his record on Tetris. He'd realized that he wasn't going to make it out of this one alive.

Just then, his phone rang. "Interrupt game?" the display asked him, in words, having already interrupted his game. It also said "Mother," the name of the person who was calling. With a sigh, he hit send, a worry shivering in him that the stewardess would come down the aisle and tell him he was interfering with the communications system. But at least then he'd get out of the bog.

"You think you're so clever, don't you," said Mother, through the door.

"Hello?" asked Clark.

"Hating the train. Locking yourself up in the toilet. Very Che Guevara."

"This is a strange business," he said to the phone, "It's like I can hear you perfectly."

"Hang up, retardo," she said. It had long been her pet name for him. "I'm right here, retardo."

He did as she said, out of ancient habit.

"How did you get up here?" he asked the door. "We're at thirty thousand feet."

She ignored him, out of ancient habit.

"Everyone hates taking the train," she said. "I don't see why you have to make such a snog and dance about it."

"Song and dance."

"What? I can't hear you if you speak like that."

"It's out of date" he repeated.

"Oh, he's a genius, he hates the train because it's out of date. Ever heard of the Wright brothers, smart arse?"

This was her other pet name for him.

"I have, I have."

"The train was superceded a long time ago, smart arse."

"I know, I know."

"So why have you locked yourself in the bathroom again?"

"Don't know."

"Don't mumble!"

"I don't know!" he yelled into his hands. "Leave me alone."

Mother's voice softened.

"We've taken some lovely train journeys. It's such a comfy way to get around, and it gives you such a nice view of things. Those lovely big windows, not like planes. Look out!" He ducked. "I mean, look out of the window. Do you remember the plastic brackets between the headrests on that Italian train? To put a bottle of wine in. Do you remember the train in the Andes when you woke up and saw the clouds, far beneath you? What are you so upset about, really?"

I have committed adultery, he thought, a nineteenth century sin.

"I suppose what disappoints me," he said collegially, "Is that to travel anywhere you have to haul your body into a kind of box that burns the ancient corpses of animals and vegetation in order to push you to another part of the planet. I just wish there was another way."

"Jesus," she said.

"What?"

"We should never have adopted you."

Now that's a bombshell.

"This hiding in the toilet, it's very childish, Clark. It's very retrograde. Very out of date."

Clark?, he thought.

He was silent. He wanted to tell her he still thought of her as his real mother, and that he'd come out in time for dinner like he always did, but she'd gone downstairs to the kitchen to argue with his father about him over lamb chops. She wanted him to be sent to boarding school.

He did hate the bloody fucking train. Not just because it had trapped him in its toilet: he hated it because it was out of date and he wanted to be absolutely modern in all things. He hated the train because he couldn't afford a car and the thought of taking a coach made him vomit. He hated it because whatever Mother said, the train was taking him to his fiancée, the lovely Darla, on whom he had cheated. Though right now the train was stopped, stuck, like Clark. He had to tell the lovely Darla he had cheated on her, or perhaps he did not. If not he'd go through every embrace with her with his secret in between them like a padded manila envelope containing a dead skunk, happy birthday. The secret welling up inside of him at every smooch and the lovely Darla asking him, each time with a touch more hostility, Why are you in such a funny mood?

If Clark had smoked, and he'd been stuck in a plane, this would have been the perfect time for a cigarette. Just thinking about a cigarette in an airplane toilet will set off the smoke alarms, that's how sensitive they are. Or so the curvy stewardess had told him, bending over sinuously, a cat, to pass him the quarter-bottle of red he wanted. But Clark didn't smoke, so that was no solution.

He wanted off the train. The whole tradition irked him. He imagined the continent, seen from the air, cobwebbed by railways, Gulliver waking up bound by millions of tiny ropes in the land of the Lilliputs. Or at least, that's how it was in Europe, Clark thought, but not in those words. In Europe, trains made sense. Trains invented time. But in North America, where this paragraph takes place, where the distances between cities are so vast, the infrastructure so pitiful, and the prices so high, let's not mince words: it's a fucking joke. You're better off taking the plane.

Oddly enough it was on a plane where his adultery had taken place. On his way to Europe, bien sur. That was the secret that was heckling him now, spreading from its parentheses, he had to tell her. Will he? The suspense is killing me. The stewardess had locked the compartment doors and drawn down the blind, as in the nineteenth century. Her slender brown forearms, crossed, pushed up her red-lace cupped breasts. Oh yes, she'd taken her top off. "Sure, the train's an out of date contraption," she said huskily, unbuttoning his trousers. "But don't dismiss it all at once. Think about the view it gives of life, the large windows, the human pace. Think of the labour that went into making this device, before you throw it away. I'd like to see you try to make one." But then she couldn't say any more because her mouth was full.

Well, the mind is its own place, thought Clark, in those words. He wondered if it was credible that in all this time no one had needed to go to the toilet. That had been his one hope, that someone would come to use the toilet, and tell the world entire entirely about his predicament. But no one had. Not one of all the hundreds of other passengers on the mile-long train had needed to go to the toilet. I hardly believe it myself. Maybe because the train had stopped. Clark didn't want to spend the rest of his brief life in the bog. There were no windows.

His fiancée, the lovely Darla, was waiting for him on the platform, heart full of pansies. She was going to be disappointed, wasn't she? Last night she went to the pictures with Erik, an old flame. But she didn't want Clark to be jealous, so she told him she was going with Fiona, a single mother friend of hers who always desperately needed to get out of the house.

With all this talk about Clark and the discussion of his thoughts and feelings I forgot to mention: when he sat down on the bog a few paragraphs up, he took his cellphone from his faded leather jacket pocket: his saviour. He started playing Tetris, trying to break his record store. Record score. Anything to avoid thinking about telling the lovely Darla his secret. Anything other than this. He'd realized that he wasn't going to get out of this one alive.

Just then, there was a pounding at the door.

"We've come to rescue you, Clark!"

Clark?, he thought.

"Who's there?"

"The fire department."

Their theme music played.

So it is North America, he felt with relief. In Europe they would have said fire Service.

There was pounding and whirring and sawing and clanging. Shouting and heaving and pouring and whamming. Punching and heaving and kicking and reaping. Clark, curious, hit pause. Then a voice. An Irishman, for the hell of it:

"Open the door now, why don't you sonny?"

Clark tried the door again, but it was as intransigent as matter. He rattled the silver knob, but it was stuck.

"I told you already," said Clark, "I'm trapped in this bloody thing. If I could open the door I would have already. I can't. I don't know why. It must be a dramatic conceit."

"Oh, tits. We can't do anything with those."

Silence. Smell.

"So you can't help?" Clark asked, all pitiable.

"Can't be done, sonny." This in a powerfully Irish accent.

"What about your axe? Don't you have an axe?"

Silence.

"I . . ." mumble, "I left it at home."

"Where?"

"In the fire engine. I left it in the fire engine!"

"You mean fire truck."

"Bien sur. I left it in the fire truck."

"Are you really a fireman?" Clark asked, all pitiable.

"Oh yes." And to Clark there came a vision of a man checking his fireman's belt and his big green fireman's helmet, to be sure.

"Oh yes," said the Irish fireman. "To be sure. Bill Pullman is playing me in the film version."

"Well listen mate, you've got to get me out of here. I've committed adultery."

"In the bog?"

"No, not in the bog. On the plane."

"Ooh the plane, sexy. Adultery's a good one and no mistake. Lucky number seven."

"Just get me out of here somehow, Mr. Fireman."

"Well we're doing all we can, but—and give me some honest feedback here—wouldn't you be better off just staying in?"

"What do you mean?"

"You've committed adultery, you're hiding in your wife's bathroom thinking about whether to tell her or not, she knows nothing, you're looking at perfumes and a tampon box, at the tiles between your feet. Just stay in. Keep it in. Keep it a secret."

Clark mulled it over.

The fireman, inspired, continued: "We get the wife here on to the plane—we have a really really big long ladder—sympathy vote for you, please come out, all is forgiven, et cet and etera."

"She's not my wife, she's my fiancée."

Silence. Smell.

"Ah well you should have said: No wife, no problem."

"Eh?"

"Adultery *means* voluntary intercourse by a married person with a person other than their spouse. No spouse, no adultery. QE2."

"But I have cheated on her."

"Ah yes, well you make a good point there."

No one spoke. Not Clark, not the fireman, not the millions tuning in on the satellite feed.

"Listen, little shamrock, wouldn't you be better off staying where you are? A sleeping dog can't lie."

"Eh?"

"Bliss is ignorance."

"You're being stupid now."

"One in the bush is worth two in the hand."

"You mean, if my being stuck in the lav represents the fact of my adultery, it should remain concealed from the lovely Darla until the end of the story? Locked away like me?"

"Something like that."

"But isn't that terribly dishonest to the lovely Darla?"

"Sure sure sure. But she did lie to you about who she went to the pictures with last night."

Clark looked at the lovely Darla's lovely blue floral shower curtain. He thought perhaps he was going to weep.

You know, it's appropriate that he was stuck where he was. It's a short piece, it all has to mean something. And it'll be over soon, I promise: the lovely Darla is on the way upstairs from her lovely kitchen already, wondering what's taking Clark so long in the bog.

As I was saying, his locking himself in there is appropriate: because in his low periods, Clark found himself paying unusual attention to his morning time in the old WC, practicing what he called excremancy. In his high periods he didn't do it, as people only trust in the horoscope when they're depressed. Now he didn't believe in such absurd notions as the Creator, let alone neurosis, but he did believe in the body: Clark believed in kidneys, lungs, his liver, things he had never seen, he believed in this physical flesh trapped in this plastic box, he believed in every atom in his lusting glands, he believed in hair and shins, in intestinal villi. It is real. So, cut to the chase, he could tell the future from his morning bowel movement. A flaky light weak poo presaged a dissolute fickle day, hard to concentrate. With corny bits. A good dark firm stool foretold a day of rewarding labour followed by a solid shag. This morning he'd been constipated. Well, what did you expect? Where better for a man with an anal fixation to be stuck?

Clark tried the door again, but it was as intransigent as matter. He rattled the silver knob, but it was stuck. He tried the door again, and then rattled the silver knob again, but he was stuck. The toilet was not a pleasant place to be. The stench coming from the U-bend was disgusting (though he could at least recognize in it his own sweet contribution), there was urine spattered toilet paper strewn around the floor, and in black ink on the door graffiti of terrifying anatomical marvels. There was very little space for him—the train might be a mile long, but he was trapped in a tiny portion of it.

Clark went back to playing Tetris, which at least had the spur of a record store to beat. Even though somewhere in his mind some part of him was thinking, I was addicted to this game in the 1980s already. It's terribly out of date.

Dearie me, poor Clark can't get a break.

He'd realized that he wasn't going to get out of this one alive.

Just then, there was a pounding at the door.

"Is it true that you committed adultery on me with a stewardess?" wept the lovely Darla, for it was she.

"Not *on* you, no."

"Against me?"

"Not *against* you, no."

"You know what I mean."

"The lovely Darla," said Clark patiently. "One stewardess, five stewardesses, what does it matter?"

"This is something you have to take seriously," she wept. "Between our bodies. If I can't trust your body, who can I trust?"

He thought, not for the first time, how strange the whole business was. Though not in these words. It was as if the sixties had passed him by. Not just the sixties, the war years too: he'd heard things had got pretty wild then, all those North American servicemen roistering around Europe. What about the Restoration? Let alone Late Roman orgies. Yes, he was starting to think that his problem with fidelity and the lovely Darla wasn't chronological.

"Look, just get me out of here and we can talk face to face," said Clark.

"It's not going to be easy," she wept.

"Believe me, I know. We'll start over. I'll be a new man. I won't lock myself in your bathroom. It's not very romantic. I'll be at the door of the plane, I mean train, I'll jump off onto the platform before it's even stopped. You'll be waiting for me with your heart full of pansies."

"I meant getting you out of the bog isn't going to be easy."

"Well, can't you try something? Isn't there a button you can push? An alarm?"

"Oh Clark," she wept.

Clark?, he thought.

"I just don't know if I can believe anything about you anymore."

"Darling the lovely Darla, we can try again."

He tried the door again, and then rattled the silver knob again, but he was stuck.

She was crying much more softly now. He had the definite feeling that he'd won her over.

"So who'd you say you went to the pictures with last night?" he asked.

But she was gone.

She was gone, the fireman was gone, the mother was gone, all the other passengers were gone, the engine driver was gone, the stewardesses were gone, the train was one big empty tube of Rolos.

"Well thanks a bloody bundle," said Clark.

He'd realized that he wasn't going to get out of this one alive.

BLIP

Adam is invited to dinner by married friends, Robbie and Claudia. He has been working in DC for two weeks. He picks up his car from the long-term lot and goes to their house straight from the airport.

They have invited a friend of Claudia's, Gemma. They talk her up before she arrives. Claudia tells him how cute Gemma is. He looks to Robbie for confirmation but gets none. Robbie tells him Gemma works at Siscore. Adam says he thinks he met her at the wedding but he isn't sure. He remembers a pale girl whose voice he could barely make out. Claudia says she thinks that must be someone else.

Claudia leaves the room—she's pregnant enough that Adam detects a slight waddle—and Robbie tells him that in February Gemma broke up with her boyfriend. Four years and now she's single. Adam raises an eyebrow.

"When I worked in London they had a word for that," he says.

"What, soft target?"

"Gagging for it."

They laugh. Robbie snorts.

Claudia comes back in, hand under belly.

"Gagging for it," Robbie repeats.

She gives them a look, and slides some red napkins onto the wooden chest that serves as their coffee table. She sits heavily and sighs and Robbie throws an arm around her. The two of them across from Adam. He and Robbie have glasses of burgundy; she reaches for her mineral water.

"So how do you know this nymphomaniac?" Adam asks.

"For god's sake you two."

"This lovely girl."

"Thank you." She sips before going on. "From McGill. But we figured out we knew each other when we were tiny. We went to the same elementary school."

"And even then she was hot."

"She's very pretty," Claudia replies. "And very smart. She's in Zurich but she's talking about coming home. I told her all about you. I told her about skiing, that impressed her." Her tone changes and she addresses them both: "She's a friend of mine Adam, she's visiting, I just thought it would be nice to have you both over, that's all."

He dips his nose into his fat wine glass, smiling because it's just a friend of hers, because Claudia and Robbie like to arrange for him to meet nice girls. Claudia has said repeatedly that since things ended with Heather he's only dated morons with more boobs than sense and it's a shame. She said she wants to be able to have him over and talk about something other than hair and TV. He likes provoking her: married people want to impose their brand of happiness on everyone else, he told her, like evangelicals, like the only way to be happy is rushing round a crib, in your flustered life.

"I got offered a job at Siscore once," he says now. "Friend of mine was there in Compliance. It's all a bit Opus Dei. Funny place. Once you're in, you're in."

"And you wanted to stay out."

They don't hire a lot of girls, he thinks.

Robbie is a big man with his friendly fleshy face above a massive sweatshirt. With his arm round Claudia and her new belly their living room is like the land of the giants. Claudia teaches medical ethics at the university; Robbie works for a money management company, evaluating mineral deposits. He's always just back from one of the *-stans* with stories of extreme vodka-drinking with local potentates in yak-skin tents. The house is full of mysterious trinkets. Since they had Rory he's been trying to travel less but it's hard. Adam would like to travel less also, or at least see some of the cities he works in, get something more than the dark bright view from the taxi window at 2 a.m., out of one eye, feeling too tired to feel anything. Wondering vaguely if he's being taken to his hotel or not.

Robbie has a display table with his collection of old military medals and ribbons under glass in the front hallway. Adam doesn't like their home very much. His own taste is starker, though since he's barely seen his apartment this year it's hard to prove what his own taste really is. He doesn't like this set up, with the living room on the main floor and the kitchen down a flight of stairs. It opens out onto their back garden but you have to traipse up and down the stairs; it's impractical. He's irked by the giant baby carriage at the door, the photo from the ultrasound in a neon frame on the mantelpiece. What a way to live, he thinks.

He decides he wants her to like him, whoever she is. Perhaps because of Siscore. "We are one of the world's largest private companies." Perhaps to show them what a nice guy he can be. Just to win her over.

He can only give her seven out of ten. Her body is fine; it's because he doesn't like her face. He does like the ashy blonde hair, long and simple; he does like how slim she is, because he always likes a girl he can wrap up in one arm. Her lips are colourless; she's wearing a thick grey skirt. He can look away from her face without feeling any loss. Normally he won't take anything less than an 8.

All this he calculates as she kisses Robbie and Claudia hello, tells Claudia to sit, sit, takes off her chequered overcoat. Shining silver blouse. Slim, small, but with unexpected pockets of curves. Fishnet tights: nice touch.

She's a sweet girl, and she's nerveless with Robbie and Claudia, and then nervous talking to him. She asks him a little about his job and when he tells her about the firm and the consulting engagements and how much he travels she nods quickly each time, and he can tell she's already heard all about him. He makes his usual charming complaints about working too much and she laughs in agreement.

They're interrupted. She spends a long time talking to Claudia about the baby on the way. He and Robbie listen; then Claudia takes her upstairs to see Rory, who Gemma says she's totally in love with. He watches her little ass glide up and away from him and wonders how it will be to have her lying beneath him.

As they drop backwards onto the low bench for dinner he asks her if she knows his friend at Siscore. He says he's not sure if Rodney is still around. But he's lucky; she works down the hall from him. She's surprised that they know each other: "We were at Princeton together," he says. He tells her the story of Rodney taking mushrooms, ground up with espresso beans, to have the juice to do a macroeconomics project between three and six a.m.. Her plain face shines with interest, she says she can't wait to confront Rodney with the evidence, and they all laugh, and she bends closer. They are very near to each other on the bench, he can see her constantly in his peripheral vision. She's let him in to a higher circle of acquaintance. He takes his time.

They praise Claudia for the soup. Gemma asks where she got the recipe: a friend of her aunt's in Rome. There's a grotto feeling to eating under a staircase. They pass two bottles of wine around in opposite directions. Adam gets Gemma talking about what a typical day is like in her Zurich office. Sometimes she buys a ship's cargo in mid-journey and turns it halfway around the world. He listens without showing off that he's a good listener; he asks professional questions without interrogating her. When it's his turn to speak he does it freely but without going on. Claudia watches them proudly, like a village matchmaker.

He sits back so as not to monopolize her. Her pupils are wide: he feels he's done enough. She looks across at him just lingering slightly and tells him that in fact she's thinking of quitting. She wants to go back to school to study music. Her first love. Claudia knew nothing: she's shocked, but then pleased; she says she's heard Gemma complain too often about work, about never having time to practice. Claudia says, "So that's what you were talking about when you were saying you might be coming back."

They make jokes about money. She laughs too; she says she'll always be able to busk in the subway, if it comes to that. If someone told Adam they wanted to be a professional skier at her age he'd say it was too late. But maybe in music it's different. He keeps his reservations to himself and tells her it sounds wonderful. Her bright face is turned towards him again and like someone in doubt she asks him if he really means it, and he tells her he does. His sisters both used to play the oboe.

Robbie has said nothing in a while. The baby monitor scratches and sniffs and they all pause, and then laugh and start talking again and Robbie pours out more wine.

Upstairs he goes over to his coat pocket and takes his Blackberry to the washroom with him to check mail. But then he changes his mind and doesn't slide it out. When he comes back down the stairs, hand trailing over the exposed brick, Robbie and Claudia are talking about their cruise to Antarctica again.

"Penguins," says Adam, sliding back down next to Gemma.

The conversation veers from how to tell if someone is flirting on email to dating sites to their worst break-ups. Adam sees Claudia look carefully at Gemma; Gemma smiles back to reassure her that she's not so fragile. Robbie is telling a story. He has had two more glasses of wine than anyone else.

"This girl once nearly killed herself over Adam," he says. He finds this funny now, he coughs as he says it. "Sweet kid. Liz, Lizzie. This was at Saint Ben's. Anyway she probably wasn't all that well-balanced to begin with but fools rush in."

"Robbie," Claudia begins.

"One day he breaks up with her—inevitably—Adam is always the breaker-upper, never the break-uppee. She was pretty crazy, she used to go out looking for wolf packs in Richmond Hill to howl at the moon with. What was her dad, I remember having some conversation with him when he came to pick her up once for dinner, he told me he'd flown jets in Korea, or something. Anyway Adam breaks up with her, I sneak him out for a few drinks to buck him up, we come back to school and there's ambulances everywhere, police car, fire truck. We look at each other; we didn't even have to ask what had happened."

"Robbie," Claudia says.

"Was she all right?" asks Gemma over her.

"Fine."

"Pills," says Adam, wondering why Robbie is telling the story. "Doctors say if it's pills it's not that serious."

Robbie stretches out his eagle arms and sticks his tongue into the sky, eyes rolling up into his head. Then back to normal: "They said she had the little whatchamacallit, the painkiller leaflet in one hand and the pill bottle in the other so they'd know just what she'd taken. I think we can call this a fairly middle class suicide. Parasuicide."

Adam thinks: he is telling this story to torpedo me, he wants to make me sound like a killer. Why.

There's a scream: the baby. Instantly Claudia rushes up from the table to the stairs.

"Anyway," says Robbie, lumbering up to turn off the speaker then looking about at the plates, bulbous fat under his sagging eyes. "Anybody want anything?" He goes in search of another bottle.

"I'm sorry," says Gemma, quietly, right next to him.

"It's a long time ago." She doesn't say anything and he adds, "We were kids."

"It's still hard though, anything like that."

He nods, but he doesn't mean it. He says nothing. Let her think he's remembering counselling interviews or rainy tearful nights, let her think there are hidden shoals of sensitivity inside him. He is thinking: Robbie has only been with Claudia, he's only ever known the one woman. Claudia left him five times, once when they were already engaged, but she came back six. For some reason, he thinks, Robbie doesn't like me succeeding with this girl, like we're back in school and he doesn't have a girlfriend. Simmering resentment of the husband for the bachelor.

Suddenly she puts her hand on his forearm, she grips a little tightly. Still he doesn't look up. The delicate silver bracelet on her wrist. It was almost too easy, he thinks.

When Robbie reappears her hand flies up and she says she's going to help Claudia.

"She looks a little like Lizzie, doesn't she?" Robbie says, watching her go.

"Not at all."

Adam offers Gemma a ride home and she accepts. Her parents live in Oakville so she's staying at the Bazalgette for her last few days in town catching up with friends, she says. He's heard of the hotel, it opened a year ago. Driving he immediately gets confused in the warren of new streets lined with townhouses. He goes fast: there's something he's trying to shake, a lump of disappointment that's settled in him since she agreed so readily to the drive. He's not sure exactly what it is; he dispels it.

He is looking at her as they talk about movies and the car bumps and he thinks there was some debris in the road—not all the townhouses are finished—and she says "What the hell was that?" He looks in the rearview mirror and sees nothing.

"Give me a minute," he says. He gets out to make sure there isn't anything caught under the car.

There's a bag in the street some metres back. He goes to move it out of the road. In the distance a siren. It's a cat, not dead yet, its back-half wrenched to the side, lifting its head up. Reflexively he looks away, then he forces himself to look back. A white head with ginger splotches, red collar round its neck. Adam's cold breath is visible over it as he kneels and it gives up the little effort it was still making to get across the street and just lies there in shock. He hit its hind legs and destroyed them: they are twisted and flattened and the fur down on its belly is black, bloodied. It watches him, breathing shallowly, hurriedly, just in the way he'd expect, with a scratchy unnatural rasp each time. He winces. Hot vomit rises suddenly into his mouth and he swallows it back and tastes the newly acid soup again.

She leans out of the window and calls over her shoulder, "What is it?" and he calls back, "Nothing." The round red lights of his car like eyes.

He looks left and right for a garbage bag or a shovel but of course there's nothing. Only trimmed hedges and newly paved garages, bright paint on the road. There is something he should do here, he knows, this is a nice little girl's pet, there is a coin on its collar with its name, but Gemma calls out to him again. Then he's on his way back to the car. He leaves it for fate to deal with as best it can.

"Just a branch," he says, getting back in.

She says it's weird, she's really not that tired, and he suggests a drink, and he parks in the hotel's little lot. She says she's been to the bar already, it's too noisy. They go straight up to her room. They're half empty, she says in the elevator, so they gave her an apartment-style for the price of a regular room. He looks at their million reflections, aware that there's a satisfaction to all this, but not quite feeling it this time. He sets off the parts of her body he likes and concentrates on those; that helps.

In the sleek room she takes off her leather boots and he asks her if she's heard the Antarctica story before. She says, "Only about a thousand times." Out of Claudia's presence she's become less earnest, a little more sarcastic. Her voice even seems to have lost some of its softness. She makes fun of Robbie's military obsession, saying he should just have joined the Marines, save time.

Adam tells her he was in Vietnam and Laos last summer and he's insisting on taking his holiday time next Christmas to go rock climbing in New Zealand. A Kiwi friend of his gave up a job at Lehmann Brothers to start his own adventure company and he's living the best life on earth down there. He asks her where she's planning on going to oboe school.

"Oboe school?"

"Music school."

She was looking at the turquoise drinks menu and passes it to him. She says she has a few options in mind.

"Like what's that place called, Julliard?"

She smiles wryly, the side of her mouth piercing her cheek. He looks down not to see, reads Daiquiri and Caipirinha.

"I'm not sure if I'm quite at that level," she says. "And I'm more based in Europe now."

"Claudia said you were moving back."

"Claudie wants everyone to move back. It's her thing."

They talk on the couch. They talk about her break-up with her boyfriend and she's neither breezy nor bitter, she accepts that it was painful, she's trying to move on. She asks how long he's going to stay with the firm. He says if you survive three years that usually means you're staying for twenty.

He feels there is something metallic in his neck blocking the motion of his head. She is angled towards him, her slim black legs folded beneath her, knees touching his thigh. Each five minutes she is a little closer. Several times he could have kissed her, he knows it, he's done it before. He watches them come and go, these little opportunities.

She goes to the washroom and as soon as she closes the door he needs to get up. In part to examine—he stayed at a similar boutique place in Los Angeles and he thinks it was better. But really to get free of this undertow, this thing he's feeling. He wants to slice it open and look at its constituent parts; he wants to walk away from it all together. He jumps up and down lightly on the balls of his feet, angles his neck left and right.

He tries sitting in an ear-shaped cylinder woven out of basket material that he's been looking at since they arrived. He struggles awkwardly out of it, unsure if it's even a chair or not. He looks for the remote for the flat screen TV but he can't find it. He slides open the Japanese divider and looks in at the low bed with its welcoming white duvet, slides it shut. On a tiny LCD panel he lowers the fire. A soft knock and the drinks come.

When he did a supplier study for Whole Foods they had him visit a battery farm, a prison for screaming chickens. Blood and feathers: he's seen worse things than a dead cat. It isn't that. The last he heard about Lizzie after she dropped out—this is ten years ago, he reminds himself—was someone saying she'd taken up with an artist in his fifties, was living with him. All the girls called it "creepy." Occasionally she's a punchline to his stories about his dating history, but she doesn't inhabit his thoughts; it's not that. So what is it then? He is used to giving his emotions a little leeway and then reining them back in. They shouldn't run on too far without him. He counts to ten. He pictures Gemma standing in front of the mirror sucking her cheeks in, pushing her boobs together. But it's hardly the first time he's been in a room with a girl he doesn't like all that much, just because she's there.

He comes back to the couch. He has a strong urge to go. He's wearing everything he brought. Car keys in his jacket pocket. He could just go. But the washroom door opens.

There's a settled, decided look on her face, but when she leans down and kisses him his lips are dry. She unkisses and takes hold of his head and brings it against her chest and he breathes in, his face against the soft silver fabric and the harder armour of her bra and the warmth of her breasts.

Then she pulls him up and slowly starts to unbutton his shirt. He takes her wrist gently to stop her but she waves him off. She slides the screen open and pushes him into the bedroom.

"I don't want to lead you on into anything," he says.

"You're not leading me into anything," she replies behind him. She giggles.

"I shouldn't have made you like me," he inexplicably blurts.

"Shush," she says, in control.

Then his skin rises to meet hers.

Afterwards he is himself again, he feels fine.

She is sleeping and he silently gets out of bed, moving the duvet as little as possible so she won't wake, untangles his clothes from hers. He buttons up his shirt, looks out at the city in the night. There is a long rectangular mirror framed in red wood. The light is on in the other room. He looks good. There is a shaver in his glove compartment if he needs it.

He puts on his suit jacket and leaves a business card on the night table. As he does so he thinks she is watching him with one eye but he looks and she isn't. He was ready to tell her he has a morning meeting or make the usual promises about the next time she's in town but she hasn't woken. She sleeps on her front, gripping the pillow lightly, making no noise. At some point she must have got up and put on a t-shirt.

He tightens up his belt.

He decides he doesn't like her piggy nostrils.

THE STUDENT

Every time Simon attended one of Giles' seminars he ironed a shirt especially. He always got on the subway too early and was always the first to arrive, even after wandering around their neighbourhood to kill time, looking at the wedding cake houses, stepping onto lawns to get out of the path of lumbering SUVs. It was summer and it was hot all day and the sun hung in the sky until late into the evening. It was too hot for his shirt and tie and each week he tried not to sweat, each week he tried to predict what Giles had picked as the evening's topic.

Lucy always answered the door. She would offer him something cool to drink and sit too close to him on the couch. He found it hard to talk to her, surrounded by Giles' books. But she'd talk, fluidly; about her acting, her plans for September, her latest audition. She had a way of talking through pauses, stretching out her sentences like a little girl pulling gum from her mouth. She looked nothing like Giles. Conversation for her was bodily: she speared Simon with her elbows, he felt the ridges of her ribs when she pressed in close to tell him something she thought was secret.

Eventually he'd find something to say and she'd listen with wide eyes, her hands still; then she'd respond with a flood of words on a barely related subject. Her mother, Julia, would bring crackers and dip to the coffee table. Simon would smile and Lucy would ignore her. Giles would sometimes be wandering in and out by now, picking a book off the shelf and standing to check a reference, then going back out to his study. When Giles was in the room

Simon could hear the sound of his own voice. Julia made a small fuss each time the doorbell rang but Lucy sat rapt with Simon; Simon waited for Giles to return.

One week Simon asked Lucy why she never stayed for the discussion and she brightened for a moment. She had auburn hair and hands like wings. But her mother had already appeared behind her: she bent over Lucy and reminded her she had her dance class and was already late. Lucy left slowly. Seated, looking at Giles, Simon felt her standing close behind him, as Julia chatted, purse in hand.

They would be waiting for the last few latecomers. The participants at Giles' seminars were his younger colleagues and his favoured graduate students. Simon was the only undergraduate and he was aware that he was being picked out for something.

Giles had liked an essay he'd written in a survey course and had sent him a note, on thick cream paper like a wedding invitation, inviting him to this informal series. Simon wanted it to open doors: he didn't want to screw up. He wasn't drifting through his degree like some of the people he'd met in residence; going to Giles' lectures had been the highlight of his year. Simon could write essays but he couldn't speak like Giles. Giles' intellectual clarity was beautiful in itself, and he was funny, and he speckled his hour-long tours through ideas with stories about the Austrian porcelain craze, recent problems in paleontology, the all-mushroom menu available at a restaurant he'd been to in Tokyo. Simon wanted to be like him.

After Lucy and Julia left, Giles would take up position in his armchair. Chairs would have been brought in from the kitchen and one or two people would sit on the huge red rug. At this point Simon would become aware of his prized position on the couch, but he was too shy in the early weeks to offer it to anyone more senior. He sat quietly with his hands in his lap. At home, sitting by the empty fireplace, Giles was less dramatic than in the lecture theatre. He was in his early sixties, fifteen years older than Julia, who had been a student of his. He had a greying beard and a bulging face like a character actor. His voice came from some combination of Cambridge, England, and Cambridge, Mass.

Giles would look round the circle and the talk would subside. Sometimes he would read from a paper he'd brought, or a newspaper clipping; sometimes he would quote a poem. He would speak extemporaneously for close to ten minutes and Simon would feel himself getting drawn in, watching as Giles snapped open an idea and laid out its component parts like a watchmaker. The discussion would be slow to begin but it would gain speed. Simon rarely felt confident enough to say anything but his mind would hum, authors would buzz in his head, he would remember jokes Giles had made about Elvis and de Tocqueville.

One evening before she left, quietly so no one would hear, Lucy asked him out for a coffee. He was surprised and he said yes. He knew there was something going on with her and he wanted to control it, make her realize that he wasn't interested. She was beautiful in a singular way but there was something reckless about her that disconcerted him. He didn't want anything to spoil this opportunity with Giles. They met that night at a donut shop near his college, a bright yellow place he'd always avoided. She said she'd sneaked out, and got frantic at the counter when she couldn't find the cream. She led him into the glassed-off smoking section, and two men arguing in Farsi over a *Sun* looked up at them expectantly.

She didn't look at him when she spoke. She was excited and ignored his small interruptions. She launched into a story about "person A" and "person B": B was keeping A from his best work, she implied; A didn't want to hurt B, but things couldn't go on this way. He was slow to realize she was talking about her parents. B was most likely having an affair: it was the only way to explain this invitation ignored, that offer withdrawn, this journey taken, that friendship ruined. She talked on and on this way and in what she said all the slights and motivations were connected. He suddenly thought of a diagram he'd seen which claimed to illustrate the shape of the Internet: thousands of blue and red lines intersecting with each other around a few key nodes. She smoked cigarette after cigarette and the ashtray was full of stubs smudged with purple lipstick. She said he was the only one she could confide in. He didn't know what to say to her. He said he didn't understand.

She got quieter after that and kept pushing the hair back out of her eyes. Then she didn't want to go home by herself and so he accompanied her in a cab; she kept trying to take his hand and each time he slowly pried it free. After dropping her off he remembered a conversation with Julia the first time they'd met: she was asking him about his studies, his plans, and all the time with her arm round Lucy. Simon had thought she was an overprotective mother: now he thought she was trying to keep Lucy from falling. He wondered for the first time why Lucy was still living at home, why she wasn't studying anything.

That weekend Giles gave a special lecture on Poland after being elevated to University Professor. Simon was there and tagged along with the group to a picnic and champagne in Queen's Park. It was a strange place to sit and drink, surrounded by traffic on all sides, but it was too beautiful a day for a reception, someone said. Lucy arrived in a taxi from a rehearsal for a Russian play that was starting soon. She pulled Simon away from the group just as Giles was being asked about his next project. Julia looked at them warily from under her big pink hat. Lucy walked with him south towards the parliament buildings, telling him abstractedly that he was a favourite of her father's, that Giles had called him a bright boy. Something warmed inside him to hear it. She looked behind her and suddenly pushed him against a tree: he had the shock of her hot tongue in his mouth, her thin body thrusting against him. He forced her away.

That week she left him eight or nine voicemail messages a day. Cajoling, apologetic, flirtatious, angry, tearful. He came home each afternoon and listened to them standing by the kitchen counter, hoping his housemates hadn't heard them, still holding his groceries and library books and keycard, not able to let them drop.

When he arrived at the next seminar Julia answered the door. She stopped for an instant then let him in: he could see Lucy on the couch staring straight ahead. He wished that just for once he'd been late. He thought she might still be angry but when he sat he had to push her away. Julia went into the kitchen.

"I didn't know if you'd come or not," she said.

"Just another Wednesday night."

He was angry with her for derailing him. She talked hurriedly about the postal strike, about the air quality warnings. From the kitchen came the sound of Julia putting dishes away. He wanted to be straightforward with her without being hurtful. He interrupted her and said he needed to say something. She curled towards him hopefully.

"I don't come here to see you," he started. "I'm here because your dad—I don't want you to think anything, Lucy, I'm here for his seminars, you know that."

Lucy smiled at him with her finger to her closed lips and he wondered if she'd heard.

"I'm not kidding, Lucy."

She sat back.

"I know that's how we met," she said coyly.

"It's not just how we met. I never wanted you to think—I don't know where this is coming from. Maybe you don't even think I . . . you're wonderful and everything, I don't want to mislead you. I just thought you thought I was coming to see you, and I'm not, I don't want you to think that."

This was how the words came out, formal and jumbled.

"You don't want to mislead me," she said, cold. And then, in a different tone of voice, "You know before you got here I was just thinking it's perfect, you're a year older than me."

"I don't know what you mean, Lucy. I never know what you mean."

He was looking straight ahead. He turned to her; she swallowed.

"So now you don't want to mislead me?" she said.

He supported his face in his hands, his elbows on his knees.

"Maybe I should have said something at the start, I didn't know if you were—"

"You don't want to fucking mislead me?" she said, much louder, her voice catching. The clatter from the kitchen stopped. She got up from the couch and stood in front of him and he spoke looking down, tired, exasperated. He could see her feet.

"I never wanted you to think I—"

Before he could finish she slapped him, hard, and he had to cover himself as she hit at him, clawing at his skin, suddenly screaming and crying. He couldn't get a grip on her to make her stop. Then Julia was pulling her away and she fled crying down the hall to her room and Julia looked at him and began to ask him what had happened, and the doorbell rang. He went to the washroom and tucked his shirt in, examined a thin line of blood on his cheek. His heart still pounding, himself near tears.

He'd always been too shy to speak but that night at the seminar—his last—he said too much, lost disputes, lost his train of thought. Giles looked at him curiously.

• • •

The following Thursday he found himself at her opening night. He felt he shouldn't be there but he wanted to see Giles. It was impossible to call the house now and Giles never checked his email and his voicemail at the department was full. Simon thought of sending him a note but he couldn't decide what to say. Giles had made it clear that he shouldn't come to any more meetings; Simon thought he'd heard Julia's protective tone in what Giles said. But he felt they could talk it through over a glass of wine in the intermission; all might still be well.

He saw neither Giles nor Julia in the lobby and waited until the second bell before taking his seat. The theatre was two-thirds full and some of the faces seemed familiar. There were lots of middle-aged couples, some with young people with them. Most of them must be related to the cast, he decided. He scanned the program and read Lucy's bio. She was playing Helen.

There was no curtain. The stage looked like a peasant cottage. The floor was dressed like caked dried mud and there were farming tools against a wooden wall at the back. Everything was brown or grey. Some minutes passed but nothing happened except for a black-clad stagehand's appearance and disappearance: the volume of talk went down briefly then rose again. He looked round the audience to see who the prettiest girl was. The people near him were looking around too, no doubt wondering about the delay.

He opened the program again and as he did so a wailing started and he made one last unsuccessful sweep for Giles as the lights went down. A group of pipers walked out with a drummer and took a turn on the stage in low light, then sat to one side. The actors came on in kilts and bonnets. They started talking about how far it was to Moscow and the twenty thousand roubles one of them was owed. They threw in "ayes" at the end of each line and asked for wee cups of tea from the samovar. He was nonplussed. He looked at the program again but the light was too dim. On stage when they said vodka they reached for bottles of scotch. A man in the audience humphed knowingly. Some of the accents held; others meandered to England, or back across the Atlantic and down to the South.

When she came on stage the room seemed to tighten. He thought initially it was because she was the only person he recognized. It wasn't—she was at the centre of every exchange, the other actors fed off her. She moved languidly among them, a shark. He couldn't look at anyone but her. He had to remind himself what he'd said a week before.

Then she was gone again and he wasn't sure what was happening. He was confused—the peasants were crofters and some of the landowners seemed to be English. The audience laughed at each exchange though to him nothing comic seemed to be happening. They laughed when Lucy's sister-in-law slipped and when the doctor flirted clumsily with her. He didn't know if the actors were making it into a comedy or the audience were. The uncle was in love with Lucy, but she was married to someone older even than he was: was that deliberate or was the actor just old?

When she came back on stage something had changed. The doctor was energetic now and she was suddenly listless. She was slow to speak and the play sagged. He heard whispered comments around him; the seats creaked as people moved forwards and back. The doctor grew more anxious and fidgeted as she struggled with her lines. He prompted her—"You were in the conservatory then, remember?" Lucy stared blankly back at him.

She had drifted away from the table where he was trying to show her a map. Her arms were by her side: she looked like herself again, her face had lost the sharp definition, the mask of beauty she'd worn in the first act. She looked in confusion at the audience and the doctor looked at her and neither of them moved or spoke. Simon was very conscious suddenly of the program on his knee, the shush of the air conditioning, the breathing of the woman next to him.

"Look here," said the doctor. "If you look at this part of the map." He pointed. She was supposed to be standing next to him. "If you look at this part of the map." He looked out to the wings and back at the map and waited.

"Yes," he said eventually, "Yes there's much less rainfall here."

Lucy had a strand of hair in her mouth. She didn't look nervous or like she had forgotten her lines: she looked like she didn't know where she was. She was confused and breathing quickly and about to scream or escape or collapse. Simon wanted to help her, to leap up and get her off the stage. He wondered where Giles was. The man sitting in front of him looked at his wife and back at Lucy and whispered.

"The red indicates areas where there are fewer trees than there were twenty-five years ago. As you can see, all through our district we've lost forests."

The doctor was running through his lines in good Canadian. Lucy sank to her knees in her plain grey dress. After another silence the doctor came towards her and touched her shoulders and tried gently to lift her and Lucy wrenched and screamed and threw him off. The audience gasped and he staggered back and stood looking at her. No one was wondering now if this was supposed to be part of the show. Simon could hear her panicked breathing.

The actress playing the sister-in-law ran out from the wings and stopped and blinked. The doctor turned away angrily and she came to Lucy and looked up at the back of the theatre and held her. Lucy seemed not to recognize her. She had started to cry now and bent her face into her hands; Simon could see her ribs juddering through the fabric of her dress.

"Doctor," Sonia said gently, "There seems to be something wrong with Helen."

The doctor had his hand in his hair.

Simon suddenly felt that in spite of their shock, the people around him wanted to see more go wrong.

Sonia very slowly brought Lucy to her knees and embraced her. Lucy seemed to gain substance. She pressed Sonia's hands and breathed and walked compactly to the table where she waited for the doctor.

"You've put so much work into this," she said, weakly, and coughed, and said it again.

The doctor looked at Sonia, a thick vein in his neck pulsing.

Lucy leaned over the table seductively, a grey cotton curve. "You're a good man," she said, in Helen's voice.

Sonia had no place to stand. She walked slowly backwards towards the exit.

"It's all I could do in this area," the doctor said. "There's much more work to be done," he went on, returning to his Scottish accent.

At the end of the scene she picked up a glass jug and smashed it on the table edge. It crashed into pieces and water spread over the map and spilled onto the stage floor and her hands bled. She wiped the blood on her midriff, maroon stains smeared onto the dry fabric. Sonia ran towards her terrified as Lucy fainted onto the glass and the lights suddenly went black.

● ● ●

"Well philosophy *used* to be queen, but now her role is sadly diminished. And we're playing a game of catch-up, in ethics say, with technological advances, medical advances. It's one reason I call myself a political scientist these days, more and more, when they interview me for the radio and so on. Though it's quite incorrect. Because no one wants to know what a political *philosopher* thinks."

Simon had run into Giles at the door to the library and had immediately suggested a coffee and Giles, awkwardly, accepted. It was a Wednesday afternoon; three months had passed since the play. Simon had been sleepwalking through the start of the year, the new lectures and tutorials and class locations, thinking about her almost all the time. He'd been shaken by what he'd seen even more than the way she'd hit him. It didn't seem like stage fright: he'd seen Lucy fall apart. He'd become convinced that Giles and Julia couldn't see that Lucy was unwell. He had to speak to them but he didn't know what he could say.

It was hard enough just getting into contact with Giles, and then there was the problem of his motivation. He knew that if he spoke to Giles it would sound like a kind of sour grapes, he'd sound like he was angry with her for falling for him. He told himself that he felt compassion for her but he knew that the presence he missed in his life was Giles, not Lucy; he missed the seminars, he missed the feeling of being ahead, the feeling of having a future. Still he was concerned for her: she'd shown him something no one else had seen.

They'd gone to an elegant Victorian café on Harbord. Giles looked spry. Simon didn't want to bring up anything serious while walking there, so as not to be interrupted, and then didn't want to bring up anything serious until they'd sat down and ordered, then not until they each had a cup of coffee in front of them. Giles spoke sunnily the whole time as if nothing could be the matter. Simon sat rearranging the sweeteners and sugar and watching the waitress come and go, thinking it wasn't the conversation he'd expected, lacking the authority to kick it into a higher gear. He listened, becoming aware that Giles' voice was aimed somewhere at the wall above his head.

"I'm speaking in Halifax at the Annual and then there's New York in a month for the American: they want me to talk about written and unwritten constitutions. A special address, it should be quite alien. Next semester in New Haven as usual and then— thanks god," he said this looking at the ceiling, "A sabbatical. I've two books promised and I can't tell you how I need the time to think."

Giles spoke gaily, left hand waving, leaning back in the chair, and looked back over his shoulder out at the street. The waitress lingered at the table next to them: a little girl in a beautiful green felt dress was looking attentively up at her, concentrating as her father explained what kind of cake she wanted.

"Is she well?" Simon asked at last.

"Julia? Fine."

"Lucy. I was at the play."

"Really?" Giles was surprised. "When? Julia said she'd had some nerves."

Simon told him he'd been at the opening night.

"Yes, she had some jitters," Giles said. "Opening night, you know. And then that terrible accident with the glass! Such bad luck . . . I was giving a paper. What did you think?"

Simon looked up from his half-finished coffee.

Giles went on. "It's the best I've seen her. I think she could be a terrific actress if she got over the butterflies."

Next to them the man told his daughter about the history of tea: tea pickers in Assam, jasmine tea, the Boston tea party, tea leaves. Simon's attention kept straying to his story. The girl was five or six but tiny for her age, brown-haired, delicate, open-mouthed.

"It wasn't butterflies, I thought. She looked like she was breaking apart." Each word took a long time to come. Immediately the tone of each sounded wrong.

"I'm not sure I know what you mean," Giles said.

Simon scratched the white tablecloth with his nail. "She looked very bad, very unwell. I wanted to talk to you about it." It was harder than he'd expected: he couldn't look at Giles as he spoke. "The things she says about you, about Julia. I don't know if you know. It's not normal, the things she says. Have you ever thought, do you think she should be seeing someone, I mean a—"

Giles cut him off. "Lucy's always been a bit high strung. I know you and she had a misunderstanding," he said more softly, "And believe me, I don't hold it against you, not one iota."

"I mean, I don't think I ever led her to think I felt something for her," Simon tried to say. "It's not about that; I'm not talking about that. It's something about her: I don't think she's well, emotionally. Mentally." As he spoke he perceived Giles' face hardening and realized there was a great distance between them. He couldn't stop talking now. "I just want you to know, I don't know if you've seen her the way I have. It's not about us, I'm trying to—"

Again Giles cut him off. "I appreciate what you're attempting to say." He spoke conclusively and wrested back the ball. "Julia and I have known Lucy for a long time." He smiled.

Neither of them spoke.

"I'd like to come back," said Simon. "You know, to the seminar. I'd like to be involved again."

Giles stood and pushed his chair in under the table and Simon looked up at him.

"Of course. Now there's nothing happening until next summer. But do be in touch, do keep in touch." He took a ten dollar bill from his wallet and left it on the table. "I have to go, I'm afraid. Faculty meeting at four, damn thing. I did have high hopes for you, you know."

They shook hands and Giles left. Simon watched Giles through the window walk quickly away. He felt he'd violated a set of rules he hadn't known about. He wondered if this was what it had been like for Lucy growing up.

Giles didn't make it far down the street before running into someone he knew. It looked like another professor. Giles didn't fully stop and they gesticulated wildly as they spoke, caught in the sudden brief wind. Giles waved, his suit jacket blowing open around him.

Next to Simon the girl was sipping her tea with great seriousness. Her father was reading his newspaper. They looked like a couple at breakfast.

THE NORWEGIAN, OR: THE INHERENT INSTABILITY OF PRIMES

It was my birthday, and for my birthday Olive said she was going to break up with one of her other boyfriends and I could watch. Very matter of factly, in her sweet and cruel tones, leaning close to me over her low cup of Vietnamese coffee. I could picture one foot crossing back over the other. I wasn't sure I wanted Olive to break up with one of her other boyfriends, and I wasn't sure I wanted to be there when she did. But she insisted.

Olive, the stupidly sexy hygienist at my dentist's. When we first met I smelled her shampoo and Oil of Olay as she bent over me. We bantered about the little blonde kid in the corridor crying, then she caused me incredible pain. With bleeding gums I asked her for her number. She said I was in luck: she'd decided she was only dating clients. Then a few weeks of making out, with me besotted and wary. She licked my teeth.

And then there we were, on the steps of the Adoption Agency, waiting for Zoltan. Olive was smoking. This building has something of a Buckingham Palace look to it, a great grey edifice hulking over the street. You can't see in through the second and third floor windows, they've been covered over with something white. It was snowing but the snow was soft, I liked how her hair poked out of her toque. She'd lit up daintily and not offered me one. I liked to just look at her but I kept my distance because she bit. She was telling me about Zoltan, he did something with databases, he claimed he'd once auditioned at the COC, she didn't buy it. He had a triple cavity.

"Don't gawp at me, sweetie," said Olive, and breathed out smoke.

I looked at the people. I looked at black bags slung over shoulders, I looked at boots and PDAs, then back at her.

"How did you decide which one it was going to be?" I asked.

"I'm not a total amateur, you know."

Had she wanted to invite me to watch this all along, or was that last minute, when I'd told her it was my birthday? Over the mango salad?

"I've got work to do," I started to say, but she cut me off.

"No you don't."

I smiled.

But then there he was, climbing the steps towards us two at a time, jeans, black jacket, very light brown skin. Poor Zoltan. We hadn't met before. He kissed her cheek for the last time.

"What the hell happened to your hand?" Olive asked him.

"I fractured my wrist," he said sadly.

"Jacking off?"

"Mountain biking."

She tittered.

"How is it for work and stuff?"

He shrugged, and the shrug made him wince, and he started to tell her, and she interrupted him.

"Listen sweetie," said Olive, "We really need to talk. Oh wait a minute. Zoltan Ned, Ned Zoltan."

The cigarette waving between us like a sparkler.

A bit of comedy after which I shook his left hand.

This is perhaps not the best introduction to Olive, for you.

I took a step back which was meant to project the idea that I wasn't really there. Zoltan had thick eyebrows and incredibly lustrous hair tied back in a ponytail, and as snow landed on it I wondered how he'd tied it, or who he'd got to do it for him, what with his wrist.

As she started to tell him he was already nodding.

"Listen Zoltan," she said, "I just don't think it's working out between us, you know? We both know it. I'm really sorry."

He gulped, surprised, but continued to nod his head. I felt uncomfortable, I pretended I couldn't hear.

"Sorry," said Olive softly, and turned to drop her cigarette into the circular ashtray at the top of the trashcan, fixing me with a glare.

He still didn't say anything.

"You saw this coming, right? You've been wonderful, it's just that I've really been—"

Without saying a word he turned around and fled down the steps, ponytail waving.

Olive looked disappointed.

"I think that went pretty well," I said after a while.

"What an asshole. I didn't even get to tell him," she replied.

"Tell him what?"

"I'm genuinely upset! It's not easy, something like this. The least you can do is respect someone enough to hear them out. Jesus." She put her arms slenderly around my neck. "I'm sorry, it wasn't a very good present, was it."

I backed off.

"I didn't even get to do my speech," she complained. "You know, how much he meant to me, that I'm just at a point in my life where I need to be by myself for a while, that it was *too* good in a way, I needed something that *wasn't* good. All that."

Her phone rang. She fished it from her purse and lifted a blue gloved finger to say that I should wait a tick.

"Hi. Oh *hi*. No. No, that would be great. Yeah. Okay. Bye, sweetie."

She looked back up at me.

"I'm sorry sweetie, I have to run."

"Hot date?" I asked.

Then she was gone too.

I had two meetings that afternoon but the first one was can-celled so I dropped into a little photography gallery near Charlie's offices. The show was mostly doubles, twins, celebrity imperson-ators; nothing caught my eye. Then I spent most of my meeting with Rocksoft making little notes about her instead of about the brochure graphics. Charlie was telling me about greens and topes and shattering glass and I nodded, I looked up every so often.

Her shoulder length browny reddy hair. I want to kiss her shoul-der. Pale pale skin. How delectable she is and offbeat. Quirky but she doesn't make a show of it, it's not too much; I just never know what she's going to say. When she says something she's got this crazy confidence, almost arrogance. Where does it come from. She knows her own worth very well. But she says it all in that little high-pitched girl's voice, it kills me, in Christopher Walken rhythms. It's not. Really. Working out. Between . . . us? She broke his heart. He ran away. His wrist was already broken.

I drew doodles of her, not her face, I couldn't quite draw her face, but the hairline, this red line dropping to the ears, I shaded in her neck. And if we get married, I thought idly, this will be one of our stories: how you broke a man's heart in two right in front of me, to show me what you were capable of. Our kids will laugh. But when I got home there was a Norwegian sitting on my couch.

"What's this?" I said, closing the door behind me. "Who the hell are you?"

He told me he was Norwegian. He said he was moving in. I said it was ridiculous; to begin with it's a one-bedroom apartment, so there wasn't space. We'd manage, he said. He said he'd cleared it with my landlord, Otto.

"Where will you sleep?" I asked him, and he said he could sleep on the couch.

"But where will I do my work?" I said, and he asked me what work I was doing. I didn't have much of an answer to that. We looked at each other for a long moment. I still hadn't taken off my boots and they were dripping. Silence.

"So," said the Norwegian, "What do you want to do?"

"This is ridiculous," I told him. "I'm calling Otto right now."

"As you like it," he said, and sat back on the couch. He stretched out his two long arms diagonally forwards and up and yawned.

I made some tea.

"Where are you from?" I asked him.

"I'm from Norway."

"What are you doing here?"

"Here here or here in Canada?" He asked me that very quickly indeed.

"Either. No. Here in Canada."

"A study."

"A study?"

"A study."

"What about here here?"

"I was just, you know, looking for a place to stay."

And that was that.

When I'm in a bad restaurant and the waiter asks me how everything is I always say fine, even if it's inedible. I need to work on that.

"I should do some work now," I told him, hoping he'd take the hint and get the hell out of Dodge.

"Fine."

"What are you going to do?"

"Me? I'll just sit here, if you don't mind." He sat back on the couch and grinned at me. He was a huge man with bright short blond hair, he looked like he might be in the Norwegian special forces, if there is such a thing. Except for his buck teeth and his incredibly round and sad eyes and very mobile hairy grey eyebrows and general air of weakness and exhaustion. There was something fragile about him, something uncertain and quiet in spite of his good humour, maybe you could even call it childish, or rent in two.

He watched me swivel round in my businessy chair and hit a key on my Mac to revive it. I checked if there were any emails about the retouching job I'd promised would be done by that afternoon, and there was nothing, so I opened up PhotoWerke and tried to get started.

"I can't concentrate with you just sitting there," I told him after five minutes.

"You can't? Why not?" he looked hurt and I immediately soft ened up. Softy!

"It's just," I hesitated, "I'm not used to anyone being here when I'm working. It puts me off."

"But why? I'm not doing anything."

"I can hear you."

"I'm not making any noise," he said innocently, and it was true, he was not.

"Well with some sense I have, I don't know if I can hear you or feel you or what, I know you're there, I know you're just sitting there, and it's—"

"Like a bat?"

"Yes like a bat, I know you're there."

"Just nervousness if you ask me," he said as an aside.

"Well whatever it is I can't concentrate."

"This is a pretty pass," he said finally, and it was the first thing he'd said that I thought sounded lugubrious, that I thought sounded like what I thought a Norwegian should sound like, that had the tone I had always imagined dwellers of Oslo and Trond-heim using in their conversations about their oil revenues and their poor circulation. All of them spoke perfect English. Perhaps he really was Norwegian, perhaps he wasn't just saying so.

"Can't you go?" I asked.

"Where to?"

"I don't know. Out."

"But where? It's freezing," he said, and brrred to illustrate.

"Well wait in my bedroom then," I told him.

Not much of a Norwegian after all, I thought.

"Your bedroom? Are you sure?"

I tried to start work but ten minutes later I had to go and check on him. He wasn't in the chair. He was already fast asleep under the covers.

"What's this?" I cried.

"What's what?"

"You're sleeping."

"I *was* sleeping."

"You're supposed to be waiting."

"This is what I do when I wait."

"That's it," I said. "This is ridiculous. I'm calling Otto right now."

"I wish you would," said the Norwegian in a loud voice. But in a quiet voice, as if at the same time, or in an undertone, he seemed to say, "It's nothing to do with Otto. You and I agreed to this. He'll think you're mad, anyway. You call him, tell him a Norwegian's moved in."

Listening to one, two, three, four rings I walked up and down in the kitchenette, always stepping on the cracks between the tiles, wishing Otto would answer and wishing he would not.

"Otto, hi. It's Ned. I'm just calling about this Norwegian fellow you've had move in with me. I don't want to make a big fuss or anything but I was wondering, what's this all about? Anyway give me a call as soon as you can, I'm going to try your cell too."

And though of course he already had it ten times over I left my number, my voice undermined by an unusual and awful sense of the ludicrousness of the message I was leaving, and a sudden uncertainty too: had we agreed to this? Had we talked about it? I had a curious idea that we had and that I had objected, but then he had brought me round. I put the phone back in its white cradle and went back into my room, and the Norwegian was asleep again. Stretched out and deeply sleeping, snoring like a cartoon character, and that was that. .

Well, if he's asleep I might finally be able to get some work done, I thought. But of course it wasn't so easy. First, I could hear his snoring, no matter where I put my earplugs. I didn't feel comfortable closing the door on him, I don't know why.

Second, I was tense and anxious waiting for Otto to call me back. We had an odd relationship. Otto was mostly an efficient friendly landlord but once in a while he could be thoughtless. Once he'd accidentally thrown out some of my possessions, and he'd repainted my apartment walls violet and black when I'd gone away for a weekend, and he was pained and confused when I'd complained and asked him to paint them back. He was a sportsman, he was always humming, he had four different phone numbers, his heart was probably in the right place, over all. Mostly I was terrified of him but whenever I got angry he backed down immediately. It wasn't impossible he would have had the Norwegian move in with me.

I tried to remember this as I paced around, unable to work, waiting for him to call: that I didn't have to get *really* angry with him, that all I had to was sound irked and he'd probably come and pick the Norwegian up that afternoon, if that was what I wanted. I could imagine him staring at the phone now, looking at it, as if that would reveal why I'd left such an odd message. He wasn't that imaginative, Otto.

I tried to work but really I accomplished so little. I listened to the Norwegian, his tuneful inhalation, his donkeyish exhale, although at times it seemed a grunting inhale and whistling exhalation. This blissful, childish, cartoon snoring.

I paced to and fro, fro and to, I was about to wake him up and kick him out a hundred times, I waited for Otto to call, I found myself wondering what things were like in Norway, did they have many old buildings, how did you pronounce those throaty Gs, or was that Icelandic.

He slept for three hours. I was pacing the floors, literally *lost* in thought, when he reappeared, rubbing sleep from his eyes.

"What time is it?" he said.

"Seven."

"I could murder some dinner," he said meaningly.

Otto had still not called. I folded my arms and the Norwegian smiled an optimistic closed-mouthed smile, thick eyebrows raised: if he'd had a moustache it would have risen up towards his nose too.

"Nothing too elaborate," he said.

"I'll make you a sandwich," I said at last, giving in as usual.

"I don't want to be any trouble." He sat back on the couch.

"Oh it's no trouble," I said sarcastically, "No trouble at all."

He smiled the smile again.

He ate with relish the sandwich I'd made him with mayonnaise and mustard. It was a triple decker: bread turkey bread cheese tomato bread. He scrolfed down huge bites, spilling crumbs gaily onto his lap and the couch, speaking the whole time as he ate, and very grateful.

"And what are you planning on doing here?" I asked. Everything in the subsequent conversation he had to say twice, because of his chewing.

"I don't really have any plans," he repeated.

"You have to do *some*thing."

"Why?"

"Everybody has to do something."

"Oh."

"I don't really have any plans. I was just told to be with you."
He bit his tongue. He stopped chewing the sandwich morsels, realizing he had seriously slipped up. The game was on.

"Told?" I said. "Who by?"

He didn't answer and so I played it cool.

I waited.

He chewed again.

"Who?" I said, in the voice of a gentleman suggesting cigars and billiards after dinner.

He burst into tears.

There was a little bit of sandwich left and he continued to quickly eat as the tears slid down his face—easily, after a slow start—and he swallowed snot. Really he was just a child, and to be honest I almost pitied him. I went over to sit with him, on the couch, and I even put my arm over his shoulders to comfort and protect him, but he ran away from me, taking the last triangle of sandwich with him in hand, dropping the plate down on to the carpet where it did not break. He ran crying into the bathroom. But he was so gentle that he caught the door at the last minute to prevent it from slamming. I waited for him to come out. I stood by the door and heard him chewing up the last bits of turkey and wiping his mouth with his sleeve. Then I heard nothing at all, as if he'd disappeared. I decided to leave him be. I didn't knock. I was able to work, for the first time all day. The phone rang. Call display said it was Otto. I let it go to voicemail.

Soon, in spite of myself, I was thinking about him all the time. He would sleep in my bed on and off during the day, whether I was there working or out for meetings or errands, and sleep on the couch at night. When I went to bed at night my bed would be warm, sometimes, from his warming presence, and I have to admit I couldn't condemn that. Otto doesn't keep the place heated so well, he's a sportsman, he has strange Germanic notions about hardiness of body, and cold sheets were for a long time the bane of my life.

We made a bit of a life together. I was in a period where I did not have to leave the house too often except for two or three meetings a week, and I was able to postpone half and do the other half by teleconferencing, feigning flu. I could do all the work I was meant to be doing on my computer, and we spent those hours together. We didn't talk so much, he didn't tell me too much about himself, which I assumed must be down to his Scandinavian reticence, but we did look at each other, often for minutes at a time, and then we would both turn at once to look out of the window together, looking together at the same cat strolling along the same balcony and stopping and sitting to lick its shoulder.

I asked myself how he would respond to my little business ideas (mushi, that is, meat sushi; white headphones, so everyone can look like they own an iPod). I wanted to remember jokes in order to tell him. Would he smile at a pun, or would he look at me blankly, from the couch, as he so often did, blankly uninterested and yet somehow beneficent?

At times like that I would look closely at him, and he didn't notice or object, he had no self-consciousness about being looked at, no self-undermining self-awareness, and I felt as the hours passed that I'd come to know every pore in his skin. The white line on his lip that I thought must be a scar from long ago (an ancient caribou goring?); the tiny mole on the lower left part of his chin, the stubble that never seemed to grow or darken at all. It was winter and I suppose he should have been snowshoeing and jumping into saunas built above frozen lakes, shooting elk and shearing reindeer, but no, he was content to sit on the couch for hours at a time. Sometimes he would lie there and watch the snowflakes, raising a vague hand once in a while as if to catch one, through the glass. I tended to stay with him; I feared what would become of him if he went out. I thought the city would chew him up. He was very clumsy; he broke three glasses in his first three days with me, until in the end I bought plastic cups, and told him to ask me when he wanted anything to drink.

When I hung up on friends with whom I was cancelling plans I would tell them why, in my head: He needs me here; look at what happens when I go out; it's just for a little while. But the Norwegian said none of these things. I knew that there was a part of me that needed to stay with him too. I don't know why, exactly.

Olive called pretty regularly, but I could never bring myself to answer. The Norwegian would stare at the display as the phone rang (I'd taught him) and every single time as if it was the first he'd say "Who's 'O Tasty'?" in a mournful voice and I'd reply Oh, just some-one, and we'd go back to what we were doing. How did he manage to insinuate himself into my life so completely, so quickly? I can't say. When I went out at all it was regretfully and I hurried back. He seemed to do nothing all day, he didn't lift a finger in the house, and it was only through the greatest effort that I got him to flush the toilet after using it.

We did talk a lot about Olive though, in spite of everything. She kept calling and he kept asking, and once I started talking about her the subject expanded of itself and took on a hundred colours, as when universal solvent is applied to a drop of black ink on filter paper. I told him she was quirky and in fact, I surprised myself say-ing it, pretty wonderful. But pretty cruel. But very pretty. Gorgeous. Great figure. Very unusual personality. Unique in fact. I went on. I think I may have talked so much about her that she became, for him, the apotheosis of sexy women. But I can't worry about that now.

Whenever I could I stayed in but sometimes you have to go out, it's unavoidable. And though I thought I'd prepared him well enough I came back to find him pale and lifeless, in a dead faint, hand lying tightly wrapped on his despairing stomach. I'd left him a plate of Thai curry on the kitchen counter but he hadn't been able to open the microwave door. I rushed to get it and the plastic wrap had been worried, as if he'd been scratching and clawing at it hopelessly. In a panic I threw it in the microwave for a minute, rushing back to him while the plate rotated and popped. I lightly slapped his face, I stepped back, I ran to get water and sprinkled it on his cheeks. My God, I thought, what have I done? The beeping of the machine didn't wake him, but when I held the steaming orange-rich plate under his nose I thought he stirred. I held the plate close so he would bask in chilis and lemongrass and red paste and chicken and bean sprouts. It started to have an effect. First his face regained colour—this is just from smelling the food, remember—then his eyes flickered open and shut and then open again. He woke, he looked up at me gratefully, tears were in his eyes, I stroked his hair.

"Everything's sideways," he said.

I swayed back—I was sitting on the edge of the couch, at his head—and gingerly he sat up. I put the plate on the floor and as I propped him up against a cushion he gazed down at it.

"You came back," he said weakly.

"Of course I did. Of course I did," I told him. "Now, eat."

He lifted a hand but it dropped and so I dipped the spoon into the yellow liquid and raised it up, full of tofu and rice and pepper. He offered his mouth wide and I grinned and put it in deep and he smacked his lips tightly down on the spoon, which he licked clean as I withdrew it. He chewed in a hurry and gulped the food down and opened wide for more. I could scarcely move, such was the emotion.

A week later the intercom blasted, waking us from our reveries.

"I'm outside," it said, "I got bored of waiting for you to call me."

"Olive?" I said.

"Who is it?" asked the Norwegian, in that unhappy voice he put on whenever there was news.

"No one."

"Buzz me in."

"Er . . ."

"Who is it?" he said.

"Who is it?" I asked.

"It's Olive, you retard. One night only one time special appearance. Buzz me in, I'm freezing my ass off."

"Okay," I said, and pressed the red button.

"Is it O Tasty?" the Norwegian asked hesitantly.

"Up," I said, and he looked at me like I'd asked him to cut his head off for charity. "Up!"

I pulled him off the couch, though his woolly sweater seemed to give in every direction and I could barely get any grip at all. I pointed him towards my bedroom and slowly, grumbling, like a turtle, in he went.

I opened the apartment door and she put her arms around me and gave me a big smacker full on the lips.

"Cold fish," she said when, surprised, I didn't grab her. "Where have you been hiding?"

"Oh, here and there."

"Hiding from me?"

She ran her hands down my sides.

"Olive," I said, in my Don't be silly voice.

She stepped back and raised a white plastic bag from the floor.

"I'm going to seduce you," she said. "I brought Cambodian food." She went to the kitchenette to get plates. She looked for candles.

How strange it was to be with someone else! Pleasant and un-pleasant at once. A stretch, the way a holiday stretches you, and while you are in that foreign place you think that this new shape you have taken on is sure to last, though it never does. Had it been months or weeks? And how had I forgotten what a delight it was, her body, her joyful body, built for pleasure, going to the cupboards to get me salt or soy sauce, not ceasing to talk for a second as she did it, talking about boyfriends, friends, clubs, dates, comings, goings, comings. I drank the first wine I'd had in weeks, she'd brought the bottle with her, she'd decided from before the beginning just what she was going to do with me, and I lined up and paid my token and got on the rollercoaster, giddy and nervous.

"I don't know anyone like you," she said, gazing drunkenly at me over our empty stained plates, over the stack of empty poly-styrene containers, "I've never met anyone like you." I didn't know what she meant, but I enjoyed the compliment. When she leaned towards me I kissed her orange lips and twisted her down off her chair onto the floor, like a slow and gentle wrestler. After a few min-utes she switched with me and straddled me. She didn't like the hardwood floors. We still had all our clothes on. My shoulder blades got bruised by the floor's unforgiving nature.

She bent down and licked my earlobe with her pink tongue. My back arched and I grabbed her hips, my favourite part of her, where the hips meet the waist, that jewelled shape, and held them tight in both hands. She whispered, "Why don't we go somewhere more comfy?"

"Give me a minute," I said, suddenly wide awake and with a pounding in my chest. "Sit right here."

In my bedroom I opened the closet and he was not there, I looked under the table and of course he was not there, I looked up at the

skylight, absurdly. Finally I ripped the covers off the bed and there
he was, asleep. "What?" he asked in his wounded voice, without
opening his eyes.

"Shush," I instructed.

"Eh?"

"Out," I said, and pointed my thumb behind me over my
shoulder at the door.

"Huh?"

I pointed again, my thumb like an idiot hitchhiker's.

"Now," I whispered.

"What?"

"Go!"

"Where?" he complained, the adolescent. But yes, I had to
think about the answer.

He still hadn't moved and I kneeled down close to him, shak-
ing left and right a little on my haunches. "Go to the washroom.
Go there very quietly. Don't make a sound. I'll come with you.
I'll be on the lookout. Okay?"

"No."

"Okay?"

"Can I just get my things together?"

"Quiet!"

I pulled him off an item of furniture for the second time in an
evening. I was roaring drunk. We tiptoed on the carpet to my
bedroom door, and I leaned out towards the kitchen and gave the
all clear, and we tiptoed onwards and I reached the silver door-
knob, which did not give.

Lugubriously, as the toilet flushed, he said into my temple, "I
think that lady's in here."

Rushing I pushed him bodily, no easy task, into the living room
and told him to get under the couch.

"Ned?" she said, as I walked by the bathroom door.

"Yup."

"Were you just talking to someone?"

"No," I said, mystified.

She came out of the bathroom and I stood in front of her and joined my hands together at the small of her back.

"What's with the pine oil shampoo?" she said, so I put my tongue in her mouth again, seeing as it seemed to like being there.

"Hold on," she said, breaking off. "I just need my purse."

I pulled her back a bit too violently.

I rushed into the living room. I couldn't see him anywhere. There was the round table, the blue tablecloth, the pile of plates and the styrofoam, the empty glasses, the couch, the bookshelves, the TV, the ladder, and no Norwegian, thank God.

"Wait up," she said, and then she was behind me.

I was sweaty and flustered.

"Here it is," she said, and then very sweetly, "Could I have a glass of water please?" Confused I went to the kitchen. I half expected to find him in the sink, or bent over and wrapped around himself like a yogi in one of the cupboards down next to the stove.

She was back on the couch now. She stood up to meet me—she curtsied when I gave her the glass, which irritated me, it was unlike her—and I saw his hand down there on the floor, pink palm up, his white wrist and then his woolly sleeve. As she swallowed water I kissed her, her lips were wet, and she squealed and I kicked his arm back under the couch and he groaned so I groaned too, hoping she wouldn't notice that the first groan was a scream of pain that had come from beneath us.

We kissed and kissed, her tongue in my mouth, then mine on top of hers, thinking about the Norwegian. She broke off and stooped and left her glass on the coffee table and then we were kissing again, and she joined her hands at the nape of my neck and pressed herself against me. Her eyes were closed. O how long you can kiss someone without getting tired of it, when you're getting to know each other. The taste of someone new, like home.

She started to pull me down but I resisted, I saw his hand creeping out towards her feet, he was going to grab her ankle. I stamped down on his palm and the hand disappeared instantly. We stood back up and I turned Olive round so I was standing behind her, she pressed her ass into me and I put my arms around her. And I kicked out under the couch, a back heel, I think I got him in the face, there was a yelp but my hands were on her breasts now, my tongue in her ear, she was sighing, she wasn't paying attention to anything else. I lowered my left hand and waved wildly behind me and to my right, meaning "Go, Go."

I pushed her forward with my crotch, guiding her with my one hand on her waist, pushing her across the living room. We took baby steps forward like pensioners with their feet tied together. Perhaps she thought I was pushing her towards the dining table, planning to bend her over it. Behind my back I continued to point and gesticulate. She said "Where are we going?" but in her voice it sounded like she liked being pointed and pushed, like a mannequin, like all her toughness obscured a desire to be shaped and modelled.

I tiptoed round her and then I was leaning my own ass against the table and she still had her back to the couch. I hoped he was getting the message. She rubbed the bulge in my jeans, hand on denim. It felt good, of course. Silently—and I must say I admired him for this—the Norwegian crept out from his hiding place and made his way towards a better one, which I hoped would be the washroom.

"Don't you have a bed?" said Olive. "I need to be horizontal."

Oh crap.

"Sure thing, baby," I answered. Kissing her neck, all the tiny hairs shining on her neck in the after dinner light. "Just let me turn the heat up in there first. It gets mighty cold otherwise."

Because though for the most part I am guileless, when required I can be quite extraordinarily cunning.

"You're so funny, all your preparations," she said sleepily, bodily.

"Sit tight," I said smiling. I led her back to the couch again.

Such choreography!

He wasn't in the washroom. Crap. He was under the covers, again. I turned on the space heater—you see, I was thinking ahead. And I bundled him out of my room into the washroom.

I smoothed down my hair and looked for a prophylactic.

"Oh man," I said. "This is going to be great. So great. Great. I can feel it."

He looked at me very blankly.

"Did you see that girl's boobs? Of course you did. Jesus fucking Christ." Through my jeans I pressed my cock against the counter.

I turned the fan on so she wouldn't hear us.

"OK," I said. "Hide in the tub."

"It's wet."

"Sorry, friend."

Slowly, reluctantly, with infinite reluctance, he meccanoed his giant thin frame into it. He had to arch his legs and he creaked over like a bridge falling. He was really much too long for it.

"Close the shower curtain," I said.

"Why?"

I turned from the sink and did it myself.

"Because it's so blue! It's just like being underwater. Like an aquarium!"

I did feel a twinge of guilt, but mostly I was thinking about taking a big bite out of Olive's lovely midriff.

I flushed the toilet, so she thought that's what I'd been doing, and then I wet my hands and dried them. I left the fan on.

"It's cold," I just about heard him say as I closed the door behind me.

She was standing in my bedroom doorway. "There you are," she said. She'd taken off most of her clothing, but she had left a little on, just enough to make me think that the stack of *Victoria's Secret* catalogues I'd accumulated as a teenager, no matter how much joy they'd given me, were really nothing, literally nothing, compared to the real thing.

I grabbed her round the waist again and felt her soft skin, and felt her soft skin through my clothes. All the blood sponging into my epidermis. She broke off and took my hand and led me into the bedroom. I thought if I turned round the bathroom door would be angled open and there'd be a hostile blue eye watching us go through the gap between the hinges. So I didn't turn round.

"What a lovely warm bed," she said, gathering the sheets around her. "Is that what you were doing, warming it up for me?"

I smiled, I pulled the sheets right off her. Just before her head crashed down onto my pillow I reached behind her and pulled a bright blond hair off the black cotton.

Sex.

I was dreaming of meeting myself in a bar and not wanting to buy myself a drink when a scream woke me. I fell back asleep again almost instantly, but then the room was suddenly bright and yellow, and I opened my eyes and they really hurt, and then she was pulling the covers off the bed furiously. I was naked.

You wake up from a deep sleep, it's the middle of the night, you're not sure quite who you are, your brain is busy doing something else, you could remake the world.

She was shaking me.

"What the fuck's going on?" she screeched hysterically.

I opened my eyes, narrowly narrowly.

She was wearing a long green t-shirt (mine) and nothing else, but that soon changed. She leaped up and started picking up all her complicated clothes off the floor and stepping into them. My head hurt and the sight of her getting dressed was a very sad one. I put the pillow over my face. It smelled like fir.

She was speaking and crying.

"Who's the fucking guy, Ned? Who's the fucking guy? I just got up to floss and—"

One pant leg, one arm in her white shirt.

"What guy?"

"The guy in the washroom!"

"The guy in the washroom?"

"The guy in the washroom."

"Oh him. He's just this Norwegian."

"You know about him? Jesus."

"What?"

She slammed the front door and I heard her clatter down the stairs.

I was so tired.

"What did you say to her?" I asked the familiar form in my bedroom door. Sleepily. I couldn't really be angry.

"Nothing," he shrugged. "Can I stay?" he said.

I was already asleep, but perhaps I nodded; I felt him lie down above the covers next to me, and then he opened them up and got into bed. I couldn't send him away, just yet.

The next evening I decided it was time for him to see a little of the city. He was very resistant. He said he didn't want anyone to know he was here, he said nobody could know, he said he was afraid of the cold and the rain and I told him it was summer, a lie. I finally said it was depressing, it was a depressing life that he was leading, that he was never going to amount to anything if he just sat on the couch all day looking at leaves falling. He said, "I don't *want* to amount to anything."

The buzzer rang.

"We're coming down," I said to the taxi driver. "You don't even have to take the subway," I said. "You won't get dirty or infected." He shuddered. "We're taking a cab."

"What if the cabbie stabs me?"

"The cabbie isn't going to stab you."

Miraculously he was in the hallway and we went down in the creaky iron lift. And there she was, it was her, Olive, waiting for us in the beautifully gentle snow. Her wet red little lips, how much I liked them, they looked crimson.

"I have guys calling me ten times a day," she said sadly, ignoring the Norwegian. She'd been crying, I thought; or perhaps it was just the cold. I sometimes cry in the cold. "Some guys. But you never call me."

"Olive," I said, about to introduce them. "Oh, I suppose you've met. Ha ha."

She nodded briskly and they shook hands. The Norwegian looked amazed, as if he'd never seen a real live girl before.

"Um. We were just going to get some Chinese food," I said clutching at inspiration, and I asked her to join us, hoping she'd say no. She said yes. "I want to see how this can work," she said.

Food.

He was playing with his fortune cookie fortune.

"It won't come true unless you eat the cookie first," she said.

He did, and then he read it out.

"It's in some crazy language," he whined.

"Turn it round," I said impatiently.

"Oh. Okay. 'You are a source of joy in others,'" he read.

"Well that's true," she grinned at him, and wiped a few yellow cookie crumbs off his chin with her napkin. "You have such strong teeth," she said amazed. "I'll clean them up for you when we get back."

I was feeling a little excluded, to be honest. All night they'd been talking fjords (it turned out she studied Nordic geomorphology in her spare time, who knew) and sagas and the conversion to Christianity and cross-country skiing. There were moments when I was so bored I felt that my head was going to split open and a baby was going to walk out with my brain in an attaché case. I was relieved that they were getting along of course, I could see that was going to make my life a lot easier, I was even thinking I was going to get Olive to come back with us for a nightcap if I could swing it. Still if we could have talked about anything I was interested in I would have been more, er, interested. I drew little pictures on the paper tablecloth, an airplane, a chauffeur's hat, a bicycle that became a man's glasses.

I paid for dinner.

That night she moved in with us.

We left the Norwegian in his spot in the tub (Olive was happy to brush her teeth with him in there, I even heard her humming) and I threw some dirty boxers under the bed and t-shirts into the cupboards and put some plates and cups into my dresser, all instanter. I looked for fresh sheets but there weren't any, I knew that already. I

should have ripped her clothes off when she came back but I needed to piss too, I didn't want that to get in my way. And brush my
teeth. By the time I got back she was already settled in bed, *perfect.*
I lifted open the black duvet and lay down beside her, it was like
clambering into behemoth's mouth, and kissed her neck and she
twittered and demurred. "Stop," she said gently, a flute dropping
down a note as she spoke.

"What," I whispered, thinking maybe she was on the rag.

"I can't," she said quietly and definitively, telling me something
I already knew.

"Why not?"

"Not with him right there. It's wrong."

I gave up instantly, I rolled backwards onto my own side of the
bed. I don't know why; I mean maybe she didn't really mean it,
maybe I could have persuaded her with a little persistence. Or maybe
I thought she was maybe right, maybe it's what I had been hoping
for her to say, in spite of myself. I thought of the Norwegian smiling in his bathtub. I felt uncertain.

We built a bit of a life together, and if this were a TV show of the
kind I used to watch when I was growing up you would see a mon-
tage, over a synthesizer melody, of me taking my boots off at the
door, of Hi honeys and the two of them leaping up from the couch
to run and give me hugs, of the three of us tobogganing gaily down
mountains and warming up over hot chocolate, of the candlelit dinner I made us all for our two week anniversary, our three grinning
faces over fondue bowls, chins and jaws red white and orange in the
flickering light. But things change, these things inevitably change, it
is the inherent instability of primes.

That morning I was busy. The Norwegian, who always woke up
early and made me a cup of tea and heated me up a croissant before

taking up his position on the couch for the day, could tell. I was already on one foot in front of my computer, trying to type as I pulled my pants on. I'd had yet another celibate night with Olive.

"What's the matter?" he asked.

Olive was still asleep.

"I've just got fourteen things to do. I've got to get to the bank, I've got a doctor's appointment, I've got to convert all these files into PDFs and send them to Harrisons, I've got two meetings scheduled at the same time," I looked at my watch, "Someone's got to go to the store and get us some food, I just don't have time to do everything."

"PDFs? I know how to do that. I can do it for you."

I didn't believe him.

"No, really," he said. "I can."

"Really?"

"Absolument."

I hesitated.

"It's no problem," said the Norwegian. "You go out. Have fun. Do your thing. Leave this," he pointed proudly, "To me."

I didn't have time to argue.

"They're in a file called Astro. It's Astro 1, 2, 3, and so on, it's sixty-five files. It might take a while."

He nodded, eyes closed, no problemo.

I wrote down the email address.

"You're a lifesaver," I told him.

He winked back at me Norwegianly.

Outside it was the worst day in the world. It was snowing a billion miles per hour and the cold flakes shot up under my useless hood into my eyes and into nose. Because of a slow old woman on the escalator I missed a train and the next one took ten minutes to arrive. The elevator in Charlie's building shut down for an hour with me in it and so I was late. The receptionist was mean to me. The meeting went badly because I was so unprepared: Charlie said he wasn't going to be feeding me any more work. On my way out I bumped into a man with a wrist cast, it was Zoltan, and it was only because I hurried away covering my face that he didn't try to stab me, I think. But hurrying away I slid on the ice and fell and hurt my knee. I slid into a puddle of slush. I didn't have any tokens and I didn't have any money so I had to walk out of the subway station again to go to a bank machine, and the ABM swallowed my card. All the human beings looked so ungainly on land, I wondered what their natural element was. I was sweaty and cold and feverish and tubercular. I was hit by lightning twice and my smarmy doctor told me the inherited genetic mutation he'd discovered in my blood test meant I was impotent, had high cholesterol and was going to have a bacterial infection in my brain tumour during a heart attack, and I'd never make any money. Because of global warming, the city slid into the lake. Then World War III began and the world ended.

Worst of all, when I got home, Olive and the Norwegian were canoodling on the couch together in front of the fire. She was reading to him, his head was on her shoulder. I didn't know who I felt more hurt by. They were curled towards each other like parentheses around nothing at all. I felt cold, colder standing there, as all my blood had drained out of my socks onto the hardwood floor and was now dripping into the apartment below.

"What's all this?" I asked.

"What's all what?" they both said at once, and giggled.

"What's so funny?" I asked.

Olive had been laughing when I came in. She looked back at the book.

"Oh nothing." He tittered, and she went on. "I just never thought of 'Library of Congress' as rude before," she said.

"Hmm . . . *congress*," said the Norwegian.

I shrugged, went about taking off my boots my coat my hat my scarf.

"Make us a cup of tea would you darling," she called out to me. "The Norwegian's very tired. *Aren't* you Norwegian? Yes you are. You *are*."

"Did you send off my PDFs?" I asked him first.

He slapped his forehead.

"Oh rats," he said. "The PDFs. I clean forgot."

I looked at the screensaver across the room, then back at the Norwegian.

Olive started tickling him, gently, grabbing at his kidneys. He squirmed and tried to keep a straight face and batted her away without really meaning it.

I stomped into the kitchenette and filled the kettle with water from the tap, not the Brita, so their tea would taste of lead. Angrily. More angry when I heard more giggling.

That night we had the conversation.

"We haven't been spending time together," I said, in bed.

My hand gently on her back moving gently up and down her soft skin.

"Sure we have," she said back to me.

"I mean alone together," in code, holding on to her a bit tighter. She didn't respond. She was far away.

"The Norwegian's so sweet," she said. "I've never met anyone like him."

"That's just what I used to think," I said curtly, then gave it one last effort.

"Don't *paw* me," she said. "I'm talking. He's like a little sweet ball, like a little ball of sweet. Where did you find him?"

I rolled back to my side of the bed.

"I told you about a million times, he just showed up. Christ."

"I don't see why you have to get all pouty," she said, calm, "I was just asking."

"Well I have told you about a million times, okay?"

"Okay," she said, her tone suggesting that it was me who was crazy. Which drove me crazy.

"Why are you always going on about him anyway?"

In the dark I could imagine her jaw tightening. I practically heard it.

"What are you talking about, Ned?"

"You do: you're always talking about him."

"What's wrong with you?" she asked, curious, not yet getting exasperated with me.

"What's wrong with *you?*"

She sighed.

"I can't deal with you when you're like this," she said.

I didn't reply.

Then out of nowhere she got emotional: "All you ever do now is snap at me. I don't understand you." This catch in her voice I'd never heard before, like tears about to come. The thick silence in the bed between us, the clogged air between us. But all I'd heard her say was *He* isn't like this.

I didn't want to move because moving could be interpreted as part of the fight. If I rolled over to her that might mean I didn't want to fight any more and anyway she could push me away. If I rolled in the other direction that could mean fuck it, I was just going to sleep. I couldn't move. But I was uncomfortable. I twisted through one hundred and eighty degrees and then I was propped up over the pillow.

"I don't know what you're thinking if you don't tell me," she said.

I'm not a mindreader, I thought.

"I'm not a—"

"Nothing. I'm not thinking anything."

Say twenty more seconds passed, and I said what I was thinking, in the full knowledge that the question was going to start major ground hostilities.

"Do you realize we haven't had sex since he showed up?"

"What?"

"Do you realize we haven't had sex since he showed up?" I repeated, very calm, as if she'd only misheard.

"Of course we have."

"That once."

"You didn't call *me*, as far as I recall."

She had me there.

"What about the first night he was here," she went on, "You didn't even tell me he existed."

But it's easy to be reasonable in the middle of being fantastically unreasonable: "Okay," I said, "Apart from that first night. Apart from that first night we haven't had sex since he arrived."

"Well so?"

"What do you mean, so?"

"Is that what this is about, sex?"

There was a knock at the door.

"What the fuck?" I said, casting about for my hockey stick.

He came into the room.

"Are you fighting?" he asked in wonderment.

"What is it," asked Olive gently. I'd discovered her extraordinary ability to change her mood, instantly, like an actress practicing expressions in her bathroom mirror. Her voice was soft again.

"You're so noisy," he said.

"Come here," she said, stretching her arms out. "Poor thing."

He leaped gleefully onto the bed.

"Push over," he said, and burped. She chided him and he excused himself.

He was on the side, then Olive, then me. She was suddenly sleepy, it seemed. I thought she must be holding tightly on to him. The two of them together, like scare marks around a quotation, and me the boring prose outside.

"Oh sweetie," she asked him, "Did you have a bad dream?"

He and I both nodded at the same time.

I lay back on my back. I sighed loudly every so often, switching to lie on my front then on my back again, pulled the duvet into disorder like a whirlpool, but she didn't get the message. I couldn't see if her eyes were open or closed, her face was turned away from me.

A few minutes passed in which I looked up at the ceiling, at the patterns made by the streetlights though the blinds, hatching and crosshatching. Trying to summarize my life I came up with scathing one-liners that would have won any argument for me. When a car drove past the white and grey lines disappeared, then scrolled along the ceiling, then were still again.

The Norwegian squirmed. Olive slid over on the bed towards me. I didn't dare touch her, I didn't even want her ankle against my shin, I slid over, and then I was perched on the very edge of the bed. With nowhere to put my one arm, it slid down at ninety degrees, and my hand touched the carpet. I brushed my knuckles back and forth on it, forth and back.

The Norwegian said he was cold, I think to himself, then he rolled over Olive, and pulled the covers away from me, and settled himself down delightedly between us. I didn't say anything, he exhaled in deep content, then he turned away from me and hugged her back. She never let me sleep like that, touching her, she said it made her feel crowded. I moved further away and I could feel myself almost falling off the bed. If I slid another inch, I thought, I'd tumble out; it seemed like a drop of hundreds of feet.

He didn't exactly kick me, but he squirmed incessantly, and his elbows were hard—he seemed so podgy but in bed he was so pointy—and I backed away, and backed away, I had to grab onto the bed not to fall off.

It got incredibly hot. His breathing became regular and hers too, and then he was snoring his comical snore again, though this time I couldn't smile at it.

One hypnogogic jerk and I was kicked clean out of bed.

I went to the kitchenette and poured myself a single malt, the tiles were cold and stuck to my feet. I put in three ice cubes which smelled of fish.

I decided that I wasn't going to sleep. I sat down on the couch with the bottle and resolved to wait until morning.

And actually it was the morning when we had the conversation.

They both came out of my room at once, as if they'd been planning it. Holding hands.

She sat down on the couch next to me, she'd put on that short silk chemise coat thing I liked, red silk, and her thighs were shining bright white. He sat down on the other side of her.

I nodded as she started to tell me.

"Listen Ned," she told me, "I just don't think it's working out between us, you know? We both know it. Sorry."

I couldn't believe it. I gulped, but I carried on nodding my head. I looked over at the Norwegian and then I waited for what else she had to say.

"I'm really sorry," she said.

She scratched her thigh and left a whiter thick line on the soft flesh.

I couldn't say anything.

She had such a gentle voice.

"You saw this coming, right? You've been wonderful, it's just I've really been—"

I stood up sharply. I couldn't bear it anymore. I knew what I had to do. I went back into my room and pulled the clothes I'd been wearing off the floor and back onto my body

"I think that went pretty well," I heard the Norwegian console her.

"I didn't get to tell him," said Olive, not crying.

"Tell him what?"

I was out in the hall now, they should have heard me, instead I heard them.

"That I'm genuinely upset. It's not easy, something like this. The least you can do is hear someone out, you know?" I saw her put her arms slenderly around his neck. I backed away.

"I didn't get to do my speech even," she complained, as I let myself out. "You know, how much he meant to me, I'm just at a point in my life where—" and I was on the stairs. There were grey marks on the carpet from other tenants' boots. Perhaps hers, perhaps his.

From the street I looked back at the building once. There was one light on on my floor. Then trudging through the snow I was on my way.

ACKNOWLEDGMENTS

Several people read earlier versions of these stories and improved them. In particular I wish to thank: Mavis Gallant, the Humber School for Writers; *My New Writing Technique is Unstoppable* (Chris Ames, Nick Garrison, Sanjay Sharma, Micah Toub); Kendall Anderson; Martha Bátiz; Louise Dennys; Matías Tarnopolsky; Julián Urman.

Special thanks to Barry and Michael Callaghan, Meaghan Strimas, and all at Exile Editions.

"Sleepy" previously appeared in *Exile, The Literary Quarterly*, and was selected for inclusion in the *The Journey Prize Stories 18*, 2006.

"The Norwegian, or: The Inherent Instability of Primes" previously appeared in *Telegraph*.

Exile Editions

info@exileeditions.com
www.ExileEditions.com

publishers of singular
fiction, poetry, drama, photography and art
since 1976